# All Dressed Up

"Here," she said, turning on the bathroom light and handing him a towel. She studied his shoulders and chest for a moment. "I'll get one of Dad's shirts. It may be a little small for you but it'll have to do."

"Hey, you don't need to —"

She closed the bathroom door on his protest. Her father had a half dozen cotton polo shirts in his drawer. She thought for a minute about Matt's coloring, selected a navy one, and returned to tap on the door. Matt opened it. He was holding the towel in one hand and wearing only his jeans. Wordlessly she handed him the shirt and fled red-faced down the stairs to find Gloria watching her with narrowed eyes.

Books from Scholastic
in the **Couples** series:

# SHOW SOME EMOTION

*by M.E. Cooper*

SCHOLASTIC INC.
New York Toronto London Auckland Sydney

ISBN 0-590-40424-5

Copyright © 1987 by Cloverdale Press. Photo: Pat Hill, Copyright © 1987 by Cloverdale Press. All rights reserved. Published by Scholastic Inc.

12 11 10 9 8 7 6 5 4 3 2 1      7 8 9/8 0 1 2/9

Printed in the U.S.A.                    01

First Scholastic printing, February 1987

# Chapter
# 1

"Hey, that's beautiful."

Pamela Green blinked and looked around. She had been concentrating so hard on her sketch of the tree that she hadn't noticed anyone approaching.

"Oh, hello," she said, spotting Brenda Austin standing just to her right. She didn't know the other girl very well, but everyone at Kennedy High School knew who Brenda was. Her stepsister Chris was the president of the student body, and her boyfriend had been president the year before. Brenda was heavily involved in volunteer work at Garfield House, the halfway house for teenagers in Georgetown where she and Pamela had met briefly during the Christmas holidays. Brenda was part of the circle of Kennedy's most active students; not a crowd Pamela was familiar with.

"I'm sorry," Brenda continued. "I didn't mean

1

to interrupt. Do you mind if I watch you work?"

"No, it's okay." The truth was that Pamela did mind, but she didn't feel she could tell Brenda that. Anyone was as entitled to sit in the quad as she was. Not too many people did it at the end of February, but they still had the right. She did her best to block Brenda from her mind and get on with her work.

Pamela frowned as she studied the sketch. Something wasn't quite right. She glanced back and forth from the tree to her pad. Then she saw the problem. She had made the building in the background too precise, too detailed. It drew attention away from the delicately interlaced branches of the tree. When she looked at the tree in the quad, she hardly noticed the building at all. She wanted to create the same effect in her sketch.

She took the ball of her left thumb and carefully blurred the lines of the building just enough to make them recognizable but indistinct, then strengthened the outline of the tree trunk to make it stand out more. Much better. She studied the pad a few more moments and decided to stop. The sun felt good on her face, but it wasn't strong enough to keep the cold from cramping her fingers. She opened the old tobacco tin she carried her art supplies in and put the stick of charcoal away, then started to close the sketchbook.

"Wait. Let me look at it close up before you put it away."

Pamela jumped. She had managed to forget that there was someone there. Was she getting to be *that* unaware of other people? It didn't seem like a very good sign. She smiled at Brenda and tilted the sketchbook at a better angle for her to see.

"I wish I could draw like that," Brenda said wistfully. "It's great, the way you know what to put in and what to leave out." She sighed. "What have you been up to, Pamela? I haven't seen much of you since we worked on the homeless campaign together in December."

For Pamela, the homeless campaign had been a conscious effort during the fall semester to get to know more of her classmates. She must have met fifteen or twenty new kids and all of them were nice, and pretty friendly. So far, though, she hadn't figured out how to follow up on the acquaintances she had made. The only change was that she smiled and waved to more people in the halls between classes. "Well, I've been pretty busy," Pamela said after a moment.

"Me, too," said Brenda. "I've been trying to coordinate the volunteer program at Garfield House. That's the reason I wanted to talk to you. I remembered that you're an artist, but I didn't realize that you were so talented. Do you spend a lot of time drawing? You must, to be so good at it."

Pamela felt her cheeks flush with embarrassment. "As much as I can," she replied. "I started when I was really little, too. My mom's an artist and my dad is a graphic designer."

"Born with a silver crayon in your mouth," Brenda said with a laugh. "I'd love to see more of your drawings sometime. Do you paint, too? I guess that's a dumb question. Most artists who draw, paint, don't they?"

Something about Brenda was so straightforward and sincere, that soon Pamela was talking with her as freely as if they had known each other since third grade. She found herself telling Brenda about her older brother Evan. "He's in his last year of art school now," she explained, "and he's doing really well. He's won five or six prizes and has his paintings picked for shows all over the East coast."

"That's terrific." Brenda seemed impressed. "It must be pretty hard on you, though. Especially since you're in the same field."

Pamela gave her a look of surprise. "Well, of course I'm really proud of him, but sometimes I do feel a little. . . ." Her voice trailed off.

"Tell me about it!" Brenda said sympathetically. "When my mom remarried a couple of years ago and we moved to Rose Hill, I discovered that my new stepsister was president of the Honor Society, the girl friend of the football team quarterback, and who knows what else. Can you imagine how I felt? Chris was also very nice and she tried hard to be my friend, but that just made it tougher for me. I had to go through some bad times before I sorted everything out and was able to be friends with her. I finally figured out that I had to do what mattered to *me* and not to worry so much about what everyone else was doing."

"Well, it's not quite like that with my brother, but I know what you mean," Pamela said with a sigh. "It's not always easy to do what's important to you, and people don't always understand. Look at my mother, for example. She lives in a little cabin in New Mexico about half the year — just her, her paints, and her canvases. I'm really proud of her, and I love the work she's doing, but I know a lot of people think it's selfish of her to leave me and my dad like that."

"How long have your parents been divorced?" Brenda asked sympathetically.

Pamela shook her head. "They're not. They're really very close. But Mom feels she has to have the right surroundings to paint, and a suburb like Rose Hill just wouldn't work for her. When I was ten or eleven we spent two weeks in New Mexico on vacation, and she fell in love with the place. She's been going back ever since, for longer and longer stays. I think Dad would like to move out and join her someday, but right now his business is here in Washington. I know it must sound like a really weird setup to you."

"No, it doesn't," Brenda said. "It must have taken a lot of guts for your mother to make a decision like that. It's too bad you can't all be together, though. You must miss her."

"Yeah, I do. But you know what else — and this is something I spend a lot of time thinking about — I'm not sure if she'd be doing such great work if Dad and I were out there with her. She really has to have a lot of time by herself, and it's not easy to get that kind of privacy with a family around. I wonder about myself — do I really want to be an artist if it means cutting myself off from everybody?"

"I don't think it has to mean that," Brenda said. "Everybody works differently, and you might not need the same kind of privacy your mother does. Anyway, I'm sure there's a happy medium where you don't have to isolate yourself totally."

"Well, maybe, but I haven't found it yet. I sometimes feel like I have to choose between my art work and having friends. Either way I lose something important."

Brenda gave a decisive shake of her head. "No, I won't go along with that. There has to be some way to put it all together. It's just a matter of thinking positively and creatively." She paused, then added, "As a matter of fact, I have a suggestion for you. How would you like to lead an art class at Garfield House?"

"Me?"

"Sure. We're right in the middle of starting a whole program of classes for the kids, and I think art is a natural. Seeing you out here sketching makes me think you'd be perfect to lead the class. What do you say?"

"Oh, I couldn't," Pamela said. "I don't know the first thing about it. I've never taught anything in my life. I'd be terrified."

"The kids are really great, and you'd have a lot of support from the other volunteers," Brenda persisted. "You might be a little nervous at first, but you'd get over it."

"But I'm not an expert or anything. Why don't you ask an art teacher to volunteer?"

"That's just it," Brenda said, placing her hand on Pamela's arm. "A professional teacher wouldn't have the right kind of relationship with these kids. Some of them have a lot of trouble dealing with grown-ups. But you're their age, they could relate

6

to you easily, and you have a special talent and knowledge to share with them."

"Well. . . ."

"Come on, Pamela, why not give it a try? If it doesn't work out, at least you'll have made the effort."

Pamela was torn. What she really wanted to do was give Brenda a flat no. The thought of standing up in front of a bunch of kids and trying to teach them to draw made her want to run home and hide under the covers. But she also remembered the way she had felt on Christmas Eve at Garfield House. Everyone had been working together, doing something significant, and having fun at the same time. She had liked that feeling of sharing important work with a whole group of people. Then there was Brenda. She seemed like someone who might become a good friend. What would she think if Pamela turned her down?

"I'll tell you what," Brenda continued persuasively. "Why don't you lead one session, then decide? Are you free this Saturday?" When Pamela, speechless, nodded, Brenda went on. "Good, I'll ask Tony to put a sign-up sheet on the bulletin board this afternoon. I'm going to be driving in on Saturday morning, and I could pick you up. How does nine sound? Too early for you?"

"No, I'm — "

"Great!" Brenda leafed through her notebook to a blank page and handed it to Pamela. "Here, give me your address and phone number, in case there's a change of plan. You're going to love working at Garfield House," she added as Pamela began to write. "And I'll be there to show you

7

around and take care of any problems that come up."

On Saturday morning, Pamela's alarm went off at seven-thirty. She swatted it off, rolled over, and pulled the pillow over her head. A couple of minutes later, her dog Angie nosed the door open and jumped up on her bed. Pamela sat up in a panic, sure that she had overslept. She was disoriented for a moment, unable to remember if it was a school day or not. Even after she pushed Angie off her chest and checked the clock, the feeling of panic refused to disappear.

Today was to be her first day of teaching at Garfield House. The art class had been on her mind for three days now, since her conversation with Brenda, and she had stayed up past midnight the night before, trying to figure out what to say and do in the first class. She had to find something that the kids could do without getting frustrated, but it couldn't be so easy that it seemed like kindergarten stuff. The worst thing she could do would be to act like some big expert who was doing them a favor by being there.

As she brushed her teeth, she scowled at her reflection. For the last couple of years she had worn her straight blonde hair down loosely about her shoulders. She liked the way it framed her face, and the length made it easy to take care of. Now she wondered if it didn't make her look a little too cute and babyish, more like twelve than sixteen and a half. How could she expect her students to listen to her if she looked younger than they did?

When she worked at home, she usually wore a favorite pair of bib overalls. They had started out blue, but now they sported paint specks of every color imaginable. She loved them because they were worn to just the right softness and had a pocket for everything she needed to carry. But she could hardly go to Garfield House wearing them. She was debating whether to wear a turtleneck or a blouse and sweater when she heard the telephone ring.

A moment later, her father called, "Pam? It's for you."

She knew as she went to the phone that it had to be Brenda. Maybe no one at Garfield wanted to take an art class. Or maybe everybody did, and Brenda was calling to say that she would have to teach two or three classes instead of one. Pamela wasn't sure which would be worse.

"Hi," Brenda said. She sounded worried and breathless. "Look, I'm sorry, something's come up. I couldn't call earlier because I didn't know if you'd be up."

"What's wrong?" Pamela asked.

Brenda took a deep breath. "One of the kids I've been peer-counseling had kind of a crisis last night, bad news from home. I've been here since early this morning and I don't know when I'll be able to get back to Rose Hill."

"That's tough," Pamela said, glancing over at the clock. It was after eight now. There wasn't enough time for her to get the bus to Georgetown. She was relieved, but also disappointed. She'd spent so much time thinking about the class. "You must be wiped out."

9

"I am. And to tell you the truth, I forgot all about picking you up until an hour or so ago. But don't worry, I managed to set something up. One of the other volunteers from Kennedy who's leading a class this morning will give you a ride. Be ready around nine-fifteen, okay?"

"Well — " She was about to suggest waiting a week to start her class when Brenda broke in.

"Oops, sorry," she said hurriedly. "I've got to run. Catch you later!"

"Sure," Pamela said to a dead phone. "Later."

# *Chapter*
# 2

Promptly at nine-fifteen, a horn beeped outside. Pamela swallowed a last mouthful of cereal, called a good-bye to her father, and grabbed her knapsack. An old Camaro was sitting at the curb, rumbling loudly. Most of the car was painted cherry red, but the front fenders and hood were a bright yellow that clashed terribly. The whole car was shaking from side to side in rhythm with the growl of the engine.

As she walked over, the passenger door opened and a deep voice called, "Pamela?"

The boy behind the wheel had dark hair and rugged, slightly lopsided features. At first she thought his expression was very intense, almost hostile, but then he met her eyes and smiled. He looked slightly familiar from around school, and she thought she might have seen him at Garfield

11

House on Christmas Eve, but she had no idea who he was.

"That's right," she said. She stopped a few feet from the car. In the backseat she could see a big metal tool box, a coil of jumper cables, and a couple of milk crates filled with greasy-looking auto parts. The front seat on her side was covered with a folded towel.

"Brenda said you needed a lift. Are you ready?" He pushed the door wider in invitation. "We're running a little late," he added. The engine gave a sympathetic *vrroom*.

The temptation to make some excuse and stay home was so great, that she hurried into the car and closed the door to avoid being overwhelmed by it.

"I hope you don't mind the seat," he said as they pulled away from the curb. "I've been doing a lot of work on this buggy and I spilled some oil on it, but the towel should keep you clean." He patted the dashboard. "I used to drive a pickup till I got this baby going. Sorry about the paint job." He flashed her another big smile and his dark eyes lit up. "You know Jonathan Preston, don't you?"

The sudden question took her by surprise. "Y-yes," she stammered. "A little. Not very well. I worked on the homeless project with him."

"Yeah, I thought so. He's a friend of mine. My name's Matt Jacobs."

"Pamela Green. But I guess you knew that already."

He shook his head. "Only the Pamela part.

Brenda was in some kind of rush when she called me. I haven't seen you around Garfield House, have I?"

"No, this is my first time, except for Christmas Eve. Do you work there a lot?"

"A couple of times a week." He fell silent as he turned onto the ramp to the interstate. He slowed down, watching his side mirror for a break in the stream of traffic, then deftly shifted into second gear and pressed down on the accelerator. The engine responded with a roar. The sudden surge of power forced Pamela back into her seat. She flinched as the Camaro swayed sharply to the left, inserting itself into a gap between two cars that was just long enough for it to fit into.

"Do you drive yet?" he asked suddenly.

She ordered her right hand to stop clenching the side of the seat. "No," she replied. "I was planning to learn this summer. Why?"

"Oh, no reason. I just wondered."

She looked over at him. He slouched in his seat, his left elbow leaning on the car door and the fingertips of his left hand lightly touching the crossbar of the wheel. One lock of dark hair had fallen forward into his eyes. She watched as he casually reached up to brush it back into place. She admired the grace of the gesture but wished he would keep both hands on the wheel.

"Will you look at that yo-yo!" he yelled with a laugh. He pointed ahead to the right. Four or five cars were waiting in the entry lane of the next on-ramp. The driver at the head of the line was leaning out his window and staring hopelessly at the solid stream of cars speeding by. "He'll probably be there all day," Matt continued as they zoomed past. "You can't wait around for an invitation if you want to get anywhere. He's got to work his way in there."

"Are you kidding? He's just being sensible," Pamela said. "You want him to risk his life by pulling into the traffic?"

"Well, he's got to make an effort," Matt said. "It just makes me mad to see so many lazy drivers out on the road."

"People can't all be great drivers like you, I suppose," Pamela said sarcastically.

"Then they ought to get better or get off the road. You know the saying, if you can't take the heat, get out of the kitchen!"

"That's just plain stupid," she said. "And it doesn't apply to driving at all." She wondered how they had gotten into this ridiculous argument.

"Okay, okay, I give up." He grinned at her, and for an awful moment she thought he was going to take both hands off the wheel and hold them over his head. "I guess us good drivers just have to watch out for the bad."

She shook her head in amazement. Where did he come off with this superior attitude? "What's the matter with you? If someone has trouble doing something, does that mean you have the right to lord it over them because you think you're better? I don't get it. What are you doing working at Garfield House with an attitude like that?"

"Leading a class in auto mechanics," he replied. "What are you doing — social work?"

Her face reddened, but she pretended not to notice the implied put-down. "I'm going to be giving an art class."

"Really?" His tone was suddenly cautious. "Are you an artist?"

"I'd like to be someday. I love to draw and paint."

"Oh."

And that was his last word until he pulled in front of Garfield House. "I'd better drop you off now," he said at that point. "It'll probably take me a while to find a parking space."

She picked up her knapsack and opened the door, then looked over at him. She wanted to thank him for the ride and to ask him where she was supposed to go, but he was looking straight ahead, obviously waiting for her to go. Well, he wasn't her idea of great company, either! She jumped out and slammed the door. She was about to turn back and thank him anyway when the Camaro roared down the narrow street. She shrugged and started up the steps of Garfield House.

The next half hour was like a bad dream. Pamela wandered aimlessly through the house. Her footsteps echoed in the long, blank-walled hallways and dusty stairwells. The few people she encountered gave her suspicious glances or refused to meet her eyes as they brushed past. Once she heard voices coming from an open doorway. She promised herself that she would go in and ask whoever she found to help her. But when she reached the door, she saw five kids sitting in a small circle in the center of the room. They looked at her with such tight, closed faces that she muttered an apology and scurried away.

She felt close to tears. Why on earth had she agreed to give the class in the first place? She should have known that Brenda would forget all about her since she was so involved in another crisis. This was no place for Pamela. It was obvious no one wanted her here. And she had better things to do with a Saturday morning than try to butt in where she didn't belong. The best thing she could do now was turn around and go home.

But how? She didn't know exactly where she was in Georgetown, much less where to catch the bus back to Rose Hill. In fact, she wasn't even sure that she could manage to find the front door.

She could see a flight of stairs at the end of the corridor. As she started toward them, a door opened halfway down the hall and Matt Jacobs stepped out, wiping oil off his hands with an orange rag. He saw her and said, "Hey, Pamela, are you done already? That was a short class."

She tried to turn her predicament into a joke, to keep him from seeing how upset she was. "So short it ended before it started," she said.

"What do you mean? Nobody showed?"

"I don't know. *I* didn't show. I didn't know where to go. And I couldn't find anybody to tell me."

"Why didn't you ask at the office?"

Her sense of frustration spilled out into her voice. "Because I didn't know where the office was, either, that's why!"

Matt stopped smiling and looked concerned. "Hey, I'm sorry," he said. "Just give me a minute and we'll go get this straightened out."

He stepped back into the room. She followed him in. She couldn't bear to let him out of her sight at that moment. Three guys and a girl were sitting around a big table. Spread out on a newspaper were dozens of metal parts that ranged in size from tiny to the size of a grapefruit. The kids looked as if they were about to work on a three-dimensional jigsaw puzzle, and their expressions said that they weren't too sure they could solve it.

"Why don't you try putting that carburetor back together," Matt said cheerfully. "I'll be back in a couple of minutes. Just remember, if you have to force it, you're probably doing it wrong."

That's true, Pamela thought. And that's why it was a mistake for me to come here.

Matt took her arm. "Let's go find Tony. He'll know where you're supposed to be."

The office was behind an unmarked door at the foot of the stairs. Matt tapped softly and pushed it open. The man sitting behind the cluttered desk was much younger than Pamela had expected. He looked up and tossed a report onto the top of a stack of papers. "Come on in," he called. "Any problems?"

"I guess," Matt said. "This is Pamela. She's supposed to be leading an art class this morning."

"Oh, right. Nice to meet you, Pamela." His smile was warm and welcoming. "When you didn't show up, we thought something must have kept you from coming today."

17

She couldn't say anything. It took all her energy to keep from crying.

Matt spoke for her. "She did show up. I brought her. But she didn't know where to go and there wasn't anybody around to tell her. When I dropped her off out front, I forgot she wasn't familiar with the place."

"Oh, no. Hey, Pamela, I'm really sorry that happened. I assumed that Brenda was taking care of you, and I guess she thought I was. We didn't give you much of a welcome, did we?"

She ordered her lip to stop quivering and tried to smile. "That's okay. Next time I'll make a reservation."

Matt and Tony smiled. Tony said, "Don't worry, we won't foul up like this again. Why don't you come with me and let's see if we can round up some of the kids who wanted to take your class."

"I'd better get back to my gang," Matt said. "They've probably invented some new kind of engine by now."

He started off down the hall. When Pamela called thanks after him, he gave her a wave without looking back.

Five people had signed up for her class, but Tony could only find two of them, a chubby blonde girl named Dinah and a tall, sullen-faced boy named Richie. Tony led them to a small room on the second floor furnished with a half dozen folding chairs and a rickety card table. Two tall windows looked out on the backyard.

"It's not much," he apologized, "but it's got the

best light of any of the free rooms. Pamela, why don't you come by after you're done and tell me what I can do to help you."

Get me out of here, she thought, half-seriously, but what she said was, "Thanks, Tony. I will. If I can find your office again."

"Right," he chuckled. "Dinah can show you the way."

After such a disastrous start, the rest of her morning at Garfield House seemed almost like fun. Dinah and Richie had both brought some of their work for her to see, and she spent the next half hour going over it with them, giving them her reactions and getting theirs. Dinah was fond of drawing slim girls in swirling gowns dancing under trees with intricate limbs, while Richie preferred dark, brooding landscapes and dark, brooding portraits. Both kids, it seemed to her, had talent.

"You know, Dinah," she said at the end of the class, "I love the way your trees and figures echo each other. It's as if the trees are dancing, too."

Dinah looked surprised. "Wow," she said, "I never saw that before, but I think you're right." She gave a self-conscious little laugh.

"Another thing I notice, though," Pamela continued, "is that the girls always have their backs to us. I have a hunch that you feel awkward drawing faces. Am I right?"

"Well — "

"Before our next class, why don't you try drawing nothing but faces. You can draw your friends, or just invent faces, whatever you like. And don't worry too much about whether they look real or not. Just think about eyes and noses and mouths and how they go together."

Dinah looked doubtful, but agreed to give it a try.

"And you, Richie," Pamela said, "why don't you — "

He broke in. "Draw figures, right?"

"Right."

"Whenever I try, they end up looking like twisted pipe cleaners," he said glumly.

Pamela smiled. "Then get some pipe cleaners, twist them into figures, and draw them," she suggested. "Lots of artists do that. Use pipe-cleaner models, I mean."

"Really?" He looked at her suspiciously. "Well, I'll try, I guess."

"Good. And both of you should feel comfortable about asking each other for help. This isn't a contest, you know. We're all trying to learn and get better at what we're doing. Me, too. I'll see you next week."

When she left the room, she found Brenda waiting for her. "I'm such a dope," Brenda burst out. "I got so involved with the crisis I told you about that I forgot all about you. You must have felt like I'd pushed you in the deep end of the pool and walked away."

"It was a little like that," Pamela admitted.

"I'm really sorry. Would it help any if I treated you to a slice of pizza on the way home?"

"Oh, Brenda. It's okay, really. You don't have to do that. Where's Matt? I never really thanked him for bringing me here."

20

"Matt? Oh, he left right after his class. He was probably in a hurry to get home and work on his car. Come on, I'm feeling faint from hunger. Even if you don't want to eat, you can at least come with me."

Pamela followed her out the door, wondering why she felt so disappointed.

# Chapter
# 3

"Okay, Cardinals, that's it from me today. Till tomorrow at noon, when you lend an ear to the songs you long to hear, this is Peter Lacey signing off."

Peter flicked off his microphone and brought up the volume on the last few lines of "My Home Town." As the red clock neared the vertical, he faded Springsteen, cued up the cassette of a sports report, and leaned back in his chair.

His throat felt as if he had been gargling with cotton balls. WKND, the school radio station, occupied three tiny, windowless rooms that had probably been meant for supply closets. On the coldest winter days they were stuffy and over-heated. The rest of the year they were stuffy and unbearably hot. Peter grabbed his can of soda, swished some around in his mouth and swallowed, then picked up a small stack of albums from the ledge near the turntable and opened the control room door.

Monica was in the record library with her back to him, replacing some of the albums Peter had used during his show. He stepped in quietly and put his arms around her. For one instant she pulled away. Then she leaned back and put her hands on top of his. He kissed her neck just below the left ear.

"Mmmm," she said, then gave him a look of alarm. Monica was an experienced DJ herself. She knew how embarrassing it could be when someone didn't remember that a mike was on.

He quickly reassured her. "It's okay. We've got some canned sports going out. No live mikes."

"In that case. . . ." She turned around and gave him a loud kiss. At that moment the outer door opened, and Karen Davis, a slender black girl who was the station's newest announcer, walked in. Her show was up next.

"Oh," she said, looking embarrassed. "Sorry, guys. You left the door open."

"Don't worry about it," Peter said with an impish grin. "It happens all the time."

Monica dug her elbow into his ribs and said, "I was just congratulating Peter on another show well-done."

"And that's not *rare*," Peter punned.

Karen caught the spirit of the exchange. "Isn't radio a great *medium*," she demanded, "and aren't we lucky to have a *stake* in it?"

"Enough, enough," Peter groaned, giving Karen a playful punch. "I have to get out of here before

23

I'm broiled alive." He wiped imaginary sweat from his brow and led his girl friend out into the hallway. "Do you have any plans for tomorrow afternoon, Monica?"

"Why, what's tomorrow afternoon?"

"Wednesday, the last word I heard." She shook a fist at him, and he said, "Okay, okay, no more jokes. I just heard about a wicked new local band called the Dial-Tones. I'm going to drop in on a rehearsal tomorrow after school to see if they're all they're cracked up to be. Maybe you want to come along?"

"Sure. I'd love to. That's a pretty dumb name, but I'm always up for hearing a new band. And anyway, don't you know I'd go *anywhere* with you?" Monica said, and gave him a quick kiss on the nose.

The Dial-Tones were getting set to rehearse in the basement of one of the old Victorian houses out near the community college. It was obvious someone had once tried to create a game room in the space. Woodgrain paneling covered the walls, a padded bar was tucked in one corner, and lamps with beer advertised on their fake stained-glass panels dangled from the acoustic-tile ceiling. But the concrete floor, heating ducts, and tiny head-high windows kept it from looking like anything but a basement room.

Monica and Peter stopped just inside the doorway to look around. The band members were setting up their gear, taping mike and instrument cords to the floor, adjusting speaker angles, and checking levels. Monica felt the first stirrings of

24

the excitement music always aroused in her. To be here like this, getting to know a band that was just starting out, was thrilling.

Peter was leaning back against the wall with his hands in the pockets of his battered leather bomber jacket. Monica thought he looked nervous and unsure of himself. She couldn't imagine why. Everybody in the local rock scene knew Peter. Even well-known professional DJs respected his knowledge, taste, and enthusiasm. And his show on WKND, even though it only reached students at Kennedy, had helped make regional hits out of at least three little-known records. Wasn't that the reason he'd been invited to this rehearsal?

A tall, handsome guy with blond hair cut short along the sides and longer at the back noticed them and strolled over. "Hey, my man," he drawled, clapping Peter on the shoulder.

"Hey, Brent," Peter said. "How's it going?"

"Not bad. We'll start cooking in ten."

"Super. Oh, this is Monica. Brent, here, sings leads and plays keyboard with the Dial-Tones," Peter explained.

Brent gave her a brief glance and the ghost of a nod before saying to Peter, "And writes songs, scrounges for bookings, and drives the van."

"And invites local high school DJs to his rehearsals," Peter added. "So, where do you want us to be?"

"Anywhere. Sit at the bar if you want. I'd better get back to work. I'll see you after the set." He turned away and went back to fiddling with his keyboards.

"Let's go sit down over there," Peter whispered to Monica. "We don't want to get in the way." Monica had never seen self-confident Peter so ill at ease. She couldn't figure it out. It seemed as if he wanted to fade into the woodwork and wished he hadn't come at all. She followed him to the bar where they each climbed up on a leather stool.

After fifteen minutes more of arranging and adjusting their equipment, the band was ready to rehearse. The drummer gave a preliminary roll, the bass player did a walking scale, and the guitarist played a few licks up the neck while Brent adjusted his mike boom to exactly the right angle. Then he nodded sharply and they launched into an upbeat number with a chorus that sounded like "Climb my oak and bend my birch/Baby, don't leave me in the lurch."

Two verses into the song, Brent stopped playing and waved for silence. "Zolly," he said to the drummer, "there was too much *ratata ratata boom* that time around. What we need is more like *diddle diddle bomp diddle bomp*, okay?" The drummer nodded. "And Si? You know when you do this?" He played a phrase on one of the keyboards. The guitarist nodded and repeated the phrase. "Right," Brent continued. "What if you lay some reverb on it, or maybe just the last half of it? Can do?"

"No sweat," the guitarist replied. He bent down to pull the effects pedal closer to his foot.

"Okay, from the top. And — "

The tune began once more. This time it sounded much better, much tighter, though try as she might, Monica couldn't pick out the new *diddle diddle bomp* or the added reverb. After the final chorus, Brent played a solo on keyboard and really wailed. The other members of the group glanced at each other and nodded in approval. Was he improvising his solo, then? She was even more impressed.

Monica had plenty of chances to appreciate the song. They worked on this or that part of it for almost half an hour, then played it through twice. By the end of the second time, she was getting tired of oaks and birches, but she had to admit to herself that she wouldn't mind hearing the song again sometime, maybe after a couple of days' rest.

After thirty-two bars of the next tune — an old blues number — the band worked over, she was bored silly. The drummer and bass player just weren't inventive enough to carry something where they showed so much. Brent's synthesizer work was solid, but his vocal included a lot of yips and moans that ended up sounding pretty ridiculous. His manner bothered her, too. He had apparently been watching a lot of Mick Jagger videos and concert footage. He had the smouldering eyes and sullen expression down, but he wasn't the actor or the acrobat that Jagger was, and it all ended up looking put on. She was also a little disturbed by the fact that he seemed to be practicing his Jagger bit for the only female in the room — her. But bothered or not, there was something compelling about his performance, and she couldn't take her eyes off him.

Brent seemed to understand that the blues didn't work. After a few attempts to improve it, he took the band through cover versions of a couple of current hits, then called a break.

Peter bounced off his seat as Brent ambled toward them. "Hey, that was great, man," he said. "That first rocker is definitely big. Don't change a thing."

"I liked it, too," Monica said. "Especially the second time around. The work you did really made a difference."

Brent didn't reply or even glance in her direction. "It's coming," he said to Peter. "Another month and we'll be in shape to cut a demo."

"A month!" Peter exclaimed. "Get it on a cassette and you'll be on the air tomorrow! I guarantee it!"

"Listen, my man, a word or two. . . ." He put his hand on Peter's shoulder and led him a couple of steps away from Monica. She felt like running after them and punching Brent, hard. She had never met anybody so rude.

Instead, she walked across the room and introduced herself to Zolly, the drummer, who looked slightly familiar. He turned out to be a Kennedy High graduate from two years before. After a barrage of do-you-know's back and forth, they uncovered two or three acquaintances in common and smiled at each other as if they were old friends. The guitarist and bass player drifted over, too. Pretty soon they were into an active discussion of favorite groups and great numbers. Si, the guitarist, even remembered listening to her show on K-100 the previous summer and complimented her on her play list.

Suddenly Brent was standing beside her. "I can tell you're someone who understands where we're trying to go," he said, fixing his heavy-lidded gaze on her. "It makes a difference, having you out there listening."

"Really?" For the first time she noticed just how handsome he really was, with his blond hair, very blue eyes fringed with long lashes, and his muscular frame. "Thanks. It's great to watch the whole process, you know, rather than just listening to what you finally worked out. It helps me understand it so much better."

"I'm glad," he said. "I want you to understand."

The other three members of the band drifted away, leaving her alone with Brent. The microphones and instruments made her feel as if they were standing at center stage. Shyness abruptly attacked her. "I, uh, I have to — " she stammered.

"We've got a gig this Friday night, and I'd like it if you could come."

"Well — "

"It'll make all the difference, to see your face out there."

"I can't really — "

"I'll hold a table and put your name on the comp list, okay?" He glanced across the room and added, "You and Peter, of course."

She couldn't manage to get out a single word. He nodded with satisfaction and turned away. "Okay, dudes," Brent said, "it's time to play some more rock and roll!" He made a short run over to his keyboards, raised both hands over his head, and brought them down in a crashing chord. The others casually plugged themselves in and joined him in a song with a driving reggae beat.

All the way home, Peter talked about how much promise the Dial-Tones had and what a super guy Brent was. Monica found herself answering as briefly as possible. She agreed that they had promise, and she could see that Brent was really talented, but something was holding back her enthusiasm. Was it just the dopey name of the group? That could always be changed. Look at all the really great bands that had started out calling themselves something different.

"I could tell Brent was impressed with you, too," Peter continued. "Especially after I told him about your stint as guest host on *Teen Beat* last summer. He told me he was sorry he hadn't heard you and to be sure to let him know the next time you're on the air."

Monica frowned. "When was that?"

"When I was talking to him during the break. He's going to get us comps to their gig this weekend, too. He likes having people in the audience who know what they're hearing."

"I know. He told me." Was that the reason Brent had gone so suddenly from ignoring her to making a big deal out of wanting her at their next gig? Because he realized that she might be someone useful to know? He had certainly seemed sincere when he was urging her to come to the gig. She and Peter both felt that Brent had a lot of talent and just might have what it took to be a star. It was rare to have this opportunity to see a new band get off the ground. But why didn't she feel more excited about it? "I'm really looking forward to seeing them perform," she added, then wondered if she really was.

# Chapter

# 4

Pamela was at the door to the cafeteria when Brenda caught up with her.

"Hi," she said, slightly out of breath. "How's it going?"

"Okay," Pamela replied warily. The sight of Brenda reminded her too much of her art class on Saturday. By Sunday Pamela had convinced herself that the class had been a total flop, and by Tuesday she had decided to drop it. This was the first time she'd seen Brenda since Saturday, so now was her big chance. But what if Brenda tried to talk her out of it?

"I've been hoping I'd run into you," Brenda said. "I still feel awful about abandoning you last Saturday."

"Forget it, Brenda. I arrived," Pamela said. "You don't have to be so down on yourself. You had a lot to deal with, and you forgot, that's all."

"I'm glad you understand. You made quite a

hit with your class. Did you know that?"

Pamela shook her head. "I couldn't really tell how it was going, but afterward I decided it was a disaster."

"Oh, Pamela, it wasn't at all." Brenda took her arm and led her to the end of the cafeteria line. "You remember Richie, don't you? Well, he's been doing nothing but sketching since Saturday. And he and Dinah have been talking up the class so much that at least six other kids are interested in taking it."

Pamela turned pale. The thought of dealing with that many kids at once was overwhelming.

Brenda must have noticed her reaction. "Oh, don't worry," she said. "For now, Tony is limiting it to the five who signed up originally. Later, if you feel you can handle it, maybe you'll let a few more in."

Pamela hardly noticed what she was selecting for lunch. Had she really had that much impact on Dinah and Richie? Now she didn't know what to do. Didn't she have some responsibility to those kids to carry on, or at least to give them some warning before she vanished? And aside from that, if she really felt that the class was going well, she would probably enjoy it a lot more. It certainly seemed that she had to give it another chance.

Still preoccupied with the question, she paid for her lunch and followed Brenda across the room to a table. Only after she sat down did she realize that they were at the table that by unwritten custom belonged to the circle of Kennedy students who were really involved in school activities and who set the tone for the whole student body. Pamela didn't even know most of them. A feeling of painful shyness came over her, as if she had just accidentally wandered into a private party.

The girl across from her glanced over and smiled at her. She had a long braid of coppery red hair and flashing green eyes and was wearing, of all things, an old cub scout shirt under a pair of pink overalls. She was talking to a tall, goofy-looking boy with dark curly hair and bright red suspenders, and a girl with long blonde hair and a serious expression.

"It's bad for school morale to have a whole block of time with nothing happening," the red-head was saying.

"There's basketball," the girl with the blonde hair said.

"Nothing other than sports, I should have said."

"How about another edition of the Kennedy Follies?" the boy with red suspenders asked. He saw the expression change on the first girl's face and quickly added, "Oops! Just a joke, Pheeb-a-rebop. Revivals don't usually have the pizzazz of the original show anyway."

"I guess that rules out a fashion show," a very tall girl further down the table observed.

"Why, Janie?" asked Brenda. "They wouldn't be the same fashions."

A circuit closed in Pamela's mind. The tall girl was the Janie who had been elected Prom Queen the year before, after being the surprise sensation of the fashion show they were talking about. Pamela remembered reading about her and her boyfriend, Henry Braverman, already on his way to being a successful fashion designer, even though he was still in high school.

The girl with red hair shook her head. "The acts in a new version of the Follies would be new, too, but why do it again? Next year, when most of us are gone, someone else can stage a Follies or a fashion show and have as much fun doing it as we did, because it'll be their first time. But it wouldn't be the first time for us."

"Who says the first time is the best?" the boy with suspenders demanded. "What about on-the-job training?"

"That's not the point, Woody," the blonde girl said. "We need something new and different to put some spark into the semester, something we haven't done before. How about a health fair?"

"Boo, hiss," Woody said. "Dull! Besides, Chris, the administration usually puts one on in April or May. Why give them unfair competition?"

"And how many students could we involve in a health fair?" Phoebe said. "What we need is something that a whole group of people can actively participate in and that the rest of the school will want to attend or watch in some way."

Two seats down from Pamela was a girl she knew slightly from history class. Her name was Diana and she was the daughter of a congressman from some state out West. She leaned forward and cleared her throat. "I know," she said. "Why don't we put on a rodeo?"

"With real horses and cows?" Janie asked.

"Sure! Irene Danberry will help us find the horses we need, and she probably knows people who have cattle. We might even be able to do it at her stable."

Brenda shivered. "Count me out, Diana. After what happened the last time we were at her stable, I don't care if I don't see another horse for the next five years." She turned to Pamela. "Last September a bunch of us were shooting a video out there and nearly got trampled by a stampeding herd of wild horses," she explained.

"Oh, yeah. I heard about that. You must have been terrified."

"I was. But Diana and her brother Bart saved the day. They managed to round up the horses before anyone got hurt."

"A rodeo might be really dangerous," Phoebe said. "Especially for kids who don't know what they're doing. And at Kennedy that would probably be everybody but you and Bart, Diana."

"So?" Woody said. "Kennedy High School presents the Amazing Einersons and Their Riproaring Rodeo! The greatest two-person show in town! Why not?"

"Aw, c'mon," Diana said, red-faced. "It was just an idea."

Woody was merciless. "I've got it," he proclaimed. "Instead of a real rodeo, we can have a pretend-rodeo. Some people could be animals and others could be riders. John Marquette would be perfect as a bull, wouldn't he? We could offer prizes for the best imitation of a bucking bronco and stuff. I know a few people who'd be really strong contestants."

It was his turn to be booed and hissed. He stood up grinning and bowed to each end of the table.

When everyone had calmed down, Brenda said, "But we still haven't solved the problem, have we?"

"What problem?" a new voice inquired. Craning her neck, Pamela could see that Jonathan Preston had taken a seat at the far end of the table. She smiled at him and gave him a wave. Pamela didn't know him well, but she had a good feeling about him from working with him on the homeless campaign.

"The annual dull spot in the school calendar," Phoebe explained. "We were tossing around some ideas for an exciting and worthwhile way to liven it up. I can't say we came up with any good ones."

Seeing a friend like Jonathan sit down at the table gave Pamela the extra ounce of daring that she needed to speak up. "I have an idea."

The others looked at her curiously. "This is Pamela, everyone," Brenda said. "She's a junior, and a fantastic artist."

All the eyes focused on her brought a flush to her cheeks and a tightness to her chest, but she forced herself to continue after introductions were made around the table. "What Brenda means is that I like to draw and paint. And I know lots of other kids who do, too, or who do sculpture or wood-carving or whatever. Why not have a school-wide art show? I don't mean an official show like the one at the end of the year, with teachers picking the best five pieces from every art class, but a student-run show, open to everyone."

A brief silence followed her suggestion, during which she wished as hard as she could for a small earthquake to open the floor directly under her chair.

Then Phoebe said, "What a great idea."

Pamela flashed her a grateful look.

"It is," Brenda said. She put a supportive hand on Pamela's shoulder. "There are a lot of really talented student artists at Kennedy."

"And all their friends will come to see the show," Woody added. "Or else."

"We could even have some special events as part of it," said Phoebe. "A mini-concert, or skits."

"Or someone actually painting a picture while everybody watches," Chris said.

Jonathan rapped on the table with his spoon. "It's been moved and seconded that we put on a student-sponsored art show at Kennedy High School. Is there any further discussion? All in favor? The ayes have it."

"It'll have to be passed by student council to be official," Chris warned.

"That's true," Jonathan replied, "but there's nothing to stop us from setting up an informal planning committee, is there? Student council doesn't meet until next Monday. By then we could have our ideas in really good shape to present to them." He looked around the table and seemed satisfied with what he saw. "Woody? You've had more experience at staging events than anyone. How about it?"

"Do I get to collect payola? Sure, I'll help."

"We ought to have somebody from *The Red and the Gold* to write this up for the paper. Sasha is bound to be too busy, but I'll ask her to suggest somebody. And of course we need an artist. Pam? What do you say?"

She had been sitting back, watching and listening. The sudden attention alarmed her. "Me?" she said, blinking. "Oh no, I couldn't. I've never really done anything like this."

"Then this is a good time to start," Jonathan said. "After all, it was your idea. That's enough for a working committee, I think. Later we can pull in more people as we get a better idea of the kind of talent we need."

Pamela glanced across the table and noticed that Phoebe's face was blank. Did she feel miffed that Jonathan had overlooked her, after she had been so enthusiastic about the idea? Pamela made a mental note to get Phoebe involved at the earliest possible moment.

The first bell rang, indicating lunch was over. As Pamela was stacking her dishes on her tray, Jonathan leaned over and said, "Can you stay after school this afternoon for a committee meeting?"

"Sure." She had been hoping for some time to paint, but it would have to wait.

"Great. Why don't we meet in the student government office then. Okay with you, Woody?"

"Sure, but I have to leave by four."

"So do I. This is just to get our toes wet and pass out some of the jobs that have to be done."

# Chapter
# 5

Jonathan was standing in the hall by the door to the student government office, wearing a khaki bush jacket and an Indiana Jones-style hat. He was talking to a girl with close-cropped ash-blonde hair who had an expensive-looking camera slung over her shoulder. They both turned as Pamela approached.

"Sorry I'm late," she said. "I had to stay after class to ask the teacher a couple of questions."

"No problem," Jonathan said easily. "Pam, do you know Dee Patterson? Dee's a terrific photographer who does a lot of work for *The Red and the Gold*. I was just telling her about our idea for an art show."

"I think it's super," Dee said softly, looking at Pamela with huge blue eyes. "Creative people need all the encouragement they can get."

"I asked Dee to join the planning committee

with us," Jonathan added, "but I haven't gotten a definite answer yet."

"Oh, do," Pamela said impulsively. Dee seemed like someone who would understand what was important and what wasn't.

Dee laughed. "I'm still here, aren't I?"

"And so are we," Jonathan said. "We'd better get moving." He saw the puzzlement on Pamela's face. "I didn't have a chance to tell you. There's another committee meeting in this office this afternoon, so we can't meet here. And Woody swore he'd faint if he didn't get something to eat, so I decided we'd meet at the sub shop. I've got a car; I can drive you home afterward."

"Great," Pamela said, though the sudden change of plans made her feel a little taken for granted. Wasn't she part of the planning committee, too? Just as she was having second thoughts about getting involved in such a time-consuming project, Jonathan said, "I'm sorry I didn't have time to check with you first, Pamela. We just decided this five minutes ago, and Woody's already on his way. Ready to go?"

A cold drizzle was falling outside as they walked across the parking lot to Jonathan's old pink convertible. "I usually keep the top down," he explained with a smile. "But I'll let you girls stay dry today."

The sub shop was a major after-school hangout for the students from Kennedy High. School pennants from years past hung from the rafters, an antique motorcycle was mounted on the back wall, and the cigar-store Indian in the far corner

41

sported an old red cap with *Cardinals* embroidered in gold on the front.

Pamela had been there a few times before, but she wasn't a regular like some of the kids. She noticed that each of the big picnic-style tables seemed to be assigned by unwritten law to a particular group of students: athletes, computer nuts, heavy metal freaks, and so on. There was only one extra-roomy booth, and that was usually occupied by the kids she'd met at lunch this afternoon.

Sure enough, as soon as they walked in, she spotted Woody standing at the booth talking to Phoebe and Chris. Phoebe was chatting with a dark-haired boy who seemed to be her boyfriend. Woody saw them and waved, then pointed in the direction of the carved Indian. "I saved a table back there," he called. "Go on and order. I'll be right over."

They left their books and coats at the table and went up to the counter. While Pamela was debating what to get, Dee ordered a small green salad without dressing, and a diet soda. Then she noticed Pamela's glance and flashed her a wry smile. "Taking it off is hard enough," Dee said, "but keeping it off is murder."

Pamela returned her smile. When the counterman asked her what she wanted, she asked for a tossed salad herself, to keep Dee company. When they carried their trays back to the table, they found Woody gloomily contemplating a hot veal parmigiana sub and a large carton of french fries.

"Sometimes I think I eat too much," he announced. "I know. For dessert I'll have a low-fat yogurt."

"You're a model of self-discipline," Jonathan said, setting down his roast beef sandwich and bag of chips.

"I know," Woody replied. "I'm pretty remarkable for my modesty, too. Are we all here?"

"This is the committee so far. Should we get right down to business?" Jonathan said.

Pamela and Dee nodded.

"Well, then, what I think we ought to concentrate on this afternoon — " Jonathan began.

"Hi, everybody," a voice interrupted brightly.

They all looked up. Dee's face tightened, and Woody frowned, but Jonathan continued to wear his usual easygoing smile. "Hi, Gloria," he said to the newcomer. "How are you?"

"Terrific. I just heard from Phoebe about what you're doing, and I had to come over and tell you what a great idea I think it is. I'm not an artist myself, but I really admire the kids who are. Most of them spend so much time with it. I really think they deserve some recognition."

Woody leaned back and tucked his thumbs under his suspenders. "I don't know, Gloria," he said. "I've always thought of you as an artist in your own way."

Her smile flickered, then returned full-strength. "Thanks, Woody," she said silkily. "I see you're just as sweet as ever." She looked back at Jonathan. "What I came over to say is that I'd really like to help out with the show. Is there anything I can do?"

"Thanks for the offer, Gloria," Jonathan said, "but I don't really know. We're just in the planning stages. As a matter of fact, you're looking at the first meeting of the planning committee. You can sit in on the meeting if you'd like. Maybe you'll have some ideas to toss in."

Pamela thought she heard a groan from Woody's side of the table, but it was covered by Gloria saying, "Oh, could I? I'd love to!" She grabbed a chair from the next table and squeezed it between Woody and Jonathan. After she sat down, she looked over at Pamela and smiled. "I don't think we've met. I'm Gloria Macmillan."

"Hi, Gloria. I'm Pamela Green."

"Pam is our artist member," Jonathan added.

"Really? That's great. I hope we get to know each other better."

"You might be better off with things as they are," Pamela thought she heard Woody whisper under his breath.

"Okay now, let's get down to business," Jonathan said. "The first thing to do is choose a place and time. It seems to me that the show ought to last for more than one day, so we have to find a place that's free for two or three days and that can be locked up during off hours. Any ideas?"

Everyone tossed out suggestions. All of the obvious possibilities — the gym, the Little Theater, the cafeteria — had obvious problems as well. Pamela tried to concentrate. She hated to think that the plan might fail for lack of a place. She waited until the others had stopped talking and said, "Do you think we could use the library?"

"How?" Gloria demanded. "They wouldn't let us hang pictures from the bookshelves, would they?"

Pamela glanced around the table, hoping that

one of the others would take over, but all she got was encouraging looks. She frowned in thought. "Well . . . what if we put a line of bulletin boards down the middle of the room? We could hang things on both sides. And we could use the ends of the bookcases, too. And they have plenty of tables; I'm sure we could borrow a couple to put sculptures on."

"No security problem," Woody contributed. "You can't take a used Kleenex out of there without signing for it first."

"But is there any chance they'd let us do it?" asked Dee. "It's not the kind of thing the administration is used to."

"That's true," Jonathan said, "but they're pretty reasonable people on the whole. Once we show them how this will bring more kids into the library and give it a more positive image, I think they'll agree. They have exhibitions in there already, after all. They're simply not *student* exhibitions."

"That's right," Dee said. "There's one up now of old engravings of Rose Hill from when it was just a country village. We had a story about it in the paper a couple of weeks ago."

"It's scheduled to last for two more weeks," Jonathan said. "After that, they don't have any more exhibits planned until the second week in April. That gives us quite a few dates, depending on how long we think it'll take us to get everything done."

"Um, Jonathan," Woody said, "how do you happen to know so much about the exhibit schedule for the library?"

"I went and asked."

"You just happened to pass the library and drop in and ask what their schedule is for the spring term?"

"Well, no, not exactly. It was pretty obvious that the library was the best space for the show — maybe the only space — so I thought I should find out whether there was any chance we could hold it there."

Pamela looked down at her plate. She had felt so happy to be able to help by suggesting the library. The discovery that Jonathan had already thought of it left her feeling like a deflated balloon.

Woody folded his arms and wrinkled his forehead. Pamela thought he looked a little like an Aztec statue. "Why have a discussion at all?" he said in an offhand tone. "You've got it all worked out already."

"That's not really fair," Jonathan protested. "I wanted to hear what everyone else had to say, too. Maybe someone would have come up with a place I hadn't thought of. And anyway, I may have had the idea of the library myself, but I didn't see how we were going to hang pictures there. Pamela solved that problem for us."

"I think it's a terrific idea," Gloria said, "whoever thought of it first. The library is just the right atmosphere for an art show. Who would want to look at a delicate painting in a smelly old gym?"

A short silence followed Gloria's comment. Then Jonathan said, "All right, we'll try for the library. The next question is dates."

After some discussion about how long it would take to publicize the show and get enough entries, they decided on the last week in March. Finally, they divided up responsibilities. Jonathan offered to talk to the administration and student government, Dee agreed to handle publicity, and everyone felt Pamela should be in charge of attracting artists. Woody volunteered to deal with the actual organization of the show.

"And what about me?" Gloria said. "What should I do?"

There was an awkward silence. No one could think of any reasonable job for her. This didn't seem to bother her, however. "Well then, I'll be sort of a member-at-large," she said breezily. "I can lend a hand wherever it's needed."

"Sure," Jonathan said with relief. "Good idea."

Pamela glanced at her watch and frowned. The meeting was running late — it was already nearly four-thirty. She wasn't going to have much time to paint before supper.

Jonathan noticed her expression and said, "Anything else we have to take care of today? I promised to give Pamela a ride home."

"Are you going in the direction of Park Heights?" Gloria asked. "Maybe you could give me a lift, too."

Jonathan agreed, but Pamela sensed some reserve in his voice. On the way to the car, she wondered why nobody seemed to be fond of Gloria.

Pamela found herself sitting alone in the backseat of Jonathan's old car. Dee had walked home to get some exercise. The rain had stopped so Jonathan put down the top of his convertible. In spite of the cold wind, Pamela found it exhilarating. She couldn't hear a word Gloria and Jonathan were saying, so she turned her thoughts to recruiting students for the show. She knew quite a few kids who she was sure would want to be involved. When they pulled up in front of Pamela's house, Gloria expressed interest in seeing her work, and Pamela ended up inviting her over to see it on Saturday morning. As she climbed out of the car she remembered her class at Garfield House. She quickly explained to Gloria, and they arranged to meet on Saturday afternoon instead.

At her door, she turned to wave, but Gloria had her head turned away and was deep in conversation with Jonathan.

# Chapter
# 6

After twenty minutes of driving aimlessly around a strange suburb a few miles north of Rose Hill, Monica and Peter finally stumbled on the Night Owl, the club where the Dial-Tones were headlining. It was at one end of a rundown 1950s shopping center, in what had once been a small neighborhood movie house. Most of the parking lot was full. Peter pulled his gold VW bug into a slot at the far end, and they walked back past the darkened shops.

Most of the places had large SALE signs in their windows. Several others were boarded up. The only lighted shop was a liquor store. As they walked by, they saw the clerk standing behind a clear, bulletproof cubicle. Peter shivered and turned up the collar of his leather jacket, and they both walked a little faster.

At the entrance to the club, Monica did a doubletake. The old ticket booth was still there, and inside it was a life-size stuffed doll in an usherette's uniform.

"Wow, she looks almost real," Peter said.

"Yeah, I was fooled for a second," Monica admitted.

Inside the double doors, from behind what had once been the refreshment stand, a very large, muscular man looked them over, took a dead cigar from his mouth, and said, "The cover's ten apiece tonight, no minimum. The first set just started."

"We're on the list," Peter said. "Monica Ford and Peter Lacey."

He ran his finger down a sheet of paper taped to the counter. "Okay," he said, looking totally unimpressed. "Go on in." He gestured with his thumb in the direction of the inner doors.

"Nice guy," Peter murmured as they walked toward the doors.

Monica was about to reply, but the flood of sound when Peter pulled the door open made it impossible. Peter leaned close to the man minding the door and shouted their names once, then again. The man nodded and motioned for them to follow him. What looked like a college crowd packed most of the room, but up front, just to the left of the stage, were four vacant tables. The doorkeeper led them through the crowd to one of these, whisked off the *Reserved* sign, and beckoned to a waitress.

"On the house," he shouted in her ear, pointing to them.

She nodded, dropped a couple of tattered menus on the tiny table, and walked away.

Monica took off her parka and draped it over the back of her chair, then sat down and slid over closer to Peter.

The Dial-Tones were playing a loud rock song with a pounding rhythm. The drums and bass were uninventive but solid, and both Si and Brent were pumping a lot of energy into their playing. They drove through the last chorus and fell silent. Brent muttered a thank you into his mike even before the applause started and moved over to confer with Zolly. Monica swallowed to clear her ears.

Peter was looking at her expectantly.

"Did you say something?" she asked.

"Yeah. Didn't I tell you they're for real?"

"Everybody seems to agree," she said, motioning at the still-clapping audience.

As the applause began to die down, Brent spoke into his microphone. "This is an old blues number called 'I Can't Keep From Crying.'" He stood poised for a moment, then he and Si ripped out three power chords, six counts of silence, and then a cascade of notes too fast to follow, leading into the vocal.

Monica glanced over and met Peter's eyes. She hadn't heard the version of this song recorded by the old Blues Project in a long time, but she realized what she was hearing now sounded just like her album at home. Si was doing a good imitation of the group's guitar player, picking out lightning-fast bent notes way up the neck. The finale met with resounding applause, cheers, and whistles.

Peter leaned closer and whispered in her ear, "Wasn't that a terrific number?"

She flashed him a grin. "Uh-huh. Too bad it wasn't their own."

"What do you mean? It's not a bad way to learn, trying to do what the greats did."

"I haven't noticed you trying to sound like Wolfman Jack lately. You've managed to find your own style."

He dropped his voice down a fifth. "This is different, Monica. Songwriting's tougher." He was about to say more but just then the band roared into action again. This time it was a tune of their own, with a driving beat and a complicated chord pattern that gave Brent and Si a chance to trade off riffs. Even Roy, the bass player, thumped out some runs that made people sway in their seats. By the last chorus, Brent was dancing back and forth across the stage, shouting the lyrics into the mike. Half the audience was on their feet stomping and dancing in time with the band.

"Wow," Monica said when the music ended. "They're really starting to get it together. That sounded fantastic."

"You're not kidding," Peter said. He was beaming and his eyes had that faraway look they got when he was beginning to lose himself in the music. "If Brent would just work on his slow ballads, he'd have it all."

Brent was scanning the audience, narrow-eyed. Monica had no idea how much he could see beyond the stagelights, but when he looked in her direction she was sure that he knew she was there.

"We're going to take a break after this next song," he said.

The crowd groaned and let out shouts of "No!"

"Don't worry, we'll be back," he added. "So stick around for the next set. Remember, we're the Dial-Tones, and we've got all the numbers!"

There was laughter and more groans, but the sounds were quickly swallowed up by the intro to another song Monica had heard at the rehearsal. Each time the chorus came around, Brent tossed his head and looked straight in the direction of their table. His heavy-lidded eyes and strong mouth drew her gaze like a magnet, and again she felt incapable of looking away.

"How do you like it so far?"

Monica looked up in surprise. Brent was standing just behind them. One hand rested lightly, possessively, on the back of her chair. She glanced at Peter, expecting to see some sign of resentment on his face. But he was beaming.

"Hey," he said, "it is really coming together. That was a great set and a wicked capper. How long am I going to have to wait for a tape I can play?"

"It'll come, my man, it'll come. We're doing a deal for some studio time right now, but we need a place with the right ambiance."

"That's super news. I can't wait to hear your demo."

Brent reached out a foot, hooked an empty chair from the next table, dragged it over, and then sat down between them. "Did you like it?"

he asked Monica, turning his back on Peter.

She nodded. "I thought the Blues Project number was very convincing."

"I'm glad to hear you say that," he replied with a smile. "We worked hard to get the right sound. What about our own material? Did we put it across?"

"Well, I think so. And as Peter said, the capper was wicked."

He smiled and placed a hand gently on her arm. "I'm glad you liked it. We've had some trouble performing that song, but tonight the mood of the crowd was just right. It helped knowing you two were here, too," he said, looking deep into Monica's eyes. "I like having friends in the audience who are already familiar with our music."

"It was a tremendous performance, man," Peter said, leaning over the table to look at Brent.

"Thanks," he said, still looking into Monica's eyes.

With an effort she turned away and looked at the stage. "The tune before the last worked really well. All the band members pulled their own weight on that one."

"You really think so? That's great to hear. It's not enough to write a song or play your part in it. We have to sound like a *band*, not just a collection of players. You think we did that better in that number than in the others?"

"I do think it had the best overall sound." She turned back and studied Brent's face. Could he really be as interested in her opinion as he seemed? At first she thought he was just doing a macho musician trip on her. That was why she had been trying so hard to seem unimpressed, to keep some sort of balance between them. But his words, and even his expression, said that he was genuinely concerned about her reactions. She was surprised to find that the more she saw of this band, the more she wanted to watch and study it. Brent really did have talent and presence. He might well be on the first rung of the ladder that led to the top. Monica had met a lot of musicians during her summer stint as a DJ. She had even interviewed some, but most of them were established already. There was something so exciting about watching a new band that was just getting started and showed so much promise.

"There's nothing ragged about your act," she continued, choosing her words carefully. "You've worked hard, and it shows. But I think you're still trying too hard to make everybody in the group seem like equals. You're holding back, and I think Si is, too. It's admirable to give everybody in the band a chance to shine, but in a band like yours, there are obvious leaders and strengths, and you should go with what feels right when you're playing. Otherwise it feels like you're stuck inside a bottle."

He flashed her a huge smile. "Kind of like we're too bottled up, you mean. Yeah, I've felt that, too."

"Well, I'm not exactly sure what I meant," she confessed with a laugh. "I thought it sounded pretty good, though."

"Maybe I can use it. 'Stuck inside a bottle, with those fizzed-up blues again.' Not bad."

"It has a familiar ring to it." Monica laughed again.

"There's an old Dylan song with a chorus sort of like that," Peter said.

Monica caught Brent's eye and they both started to laugh.

"Well, there is," Peter insisted. " 'Memphis Blues Again.' I've got it on tape at home."

"We know, Peter," Monica said tensely. "Brent was goofing on it deliberately."

"Oh. I thought maybe it was unconscious, the same way that one-seven-four rocker you played was an unconscious variation of 'Gloria.' "

Brent's face darkened, but his voice stayed level. "Well, how many chord patterns are there?" he said. "Lots of songs sound alike."

"Hey, I'm not knocking it," Peter said quickly. "Where would the Beatles have been without their Chuck Berry records? I think it's great that you've learned so much from the oldies."

"We do a lot of original material, too."

"I know, man, and I think it's fantastic."

Brent pushed himself up out of his chair. "I'd better go backstage and get ready for the second set," he said coldly. "Enjoy it, you two."

As he stalked away, Monica studied Peter's face. He looked honestly puzzled by Brent's sudden departure. Could he really be unaware that he had practically called the musician a cheap imitator and a thief?

"I'd love to be a musician," Peter said wistfully. "To take hold of people and move them like that must be the greatest feeling in the world."

"But you move people like that, too, Peter, by

56

selecting the music that fits their mood. Everybody loves your show, the way you put everything together. That's an art."

"Yeah, I guess. But it isn't the same. I live off these guys and what they create. Without me, they could go on doing just what they do, but without them, I'd be nothing. Face it, even the best DJ is a sort of musical tapeworm, but I guess I can live with that. I do like it. That's more than a lot of people can say about their work, right?" He paused, then gave her a smile that turned her heart over.

She leaned over and gave him a kiss, then leaned back in her seat and smiled. But behind her smile she felt a twinge of resentment. After all, she was a DJ, too, and a darned good one, thanks to Peter's early coaching. Did he really think of her as nothing but a tapeworm, too?

On cue, the houselights dimmed, the stagelights flared, and Brent led the Dial-Tones out to begin the second set.

# *Chapter 7*

Pamela placed her cereal bowl in the sink and took a deep breath.

"Dad?" she said. "Would you mind if I have a party here next weekend?"

She held her breath. Teaching at Garfield House and her activity on the student art show committee had convinced her that she had to do something to get to know her new acquaintances better. Throwing a party seemed like a natural answer, but the prospect terrified as much as excited her. She had never had a really big party.

Her father put down his newspaper. "Mind?" he said. "Not at all. I think it's a good idea. When did you want to have it?"

"I hadn't really — " She broke off. His quick agreement surprised her.

"I ask because I have a dinner meeting with a client on Friday that will probably keep me out of the house until after eleven." His eyes twinkled. "I hope my absence wouldn't spoil the fun."

"Oh, Dad," she exclaimed, "you know I'd love to have you here. It's just that. . . ."

"Say no more. Friday it is."

The honk outside sounded familiar. Pamela hurried to the window and smiled at the sight of Matt's waiting Camaro. It really did look like the halves of two different cars joined in the middle.

"That's my ride," she said.

"Okay, sweetheart, have fun," her father said. "Don't forget we're expecting a call from your mother this afternoon."

She wrinkled her nose in exasperation. Why couldn't her mother join the twentieth century and get a telephone installed in her cabin? Then they could talk anytime, instead of having to make all these arrangements in advance. "Don't worry," she said, "I'll be back in plenty of time."

"Good. I told you how disappointed she was to miss you last time, didn't I?"

"Yes, Daddy, you did. Several times. I had to attend an important meeting about the art show."

"I know, and I understand. This time try and be here."

"I will, Dad."

At the sound of a second beep, she said, "I'd better run. See you later." She ran out the door and down the driveway to Matt's waiting car.

"Hi," she said with a smile, slipping into her seat. "I didn't know if I'd find you or Brenda out here today."

"Didn't she call you? Tony wants her there earlier on Saturdays, so she asked me to come by for you."

"Every week?"

He seemed to interpret her surprise as a rebuff. "I guess you can work out something different with her if you want," he said, pulling away from the curb with a jolt and a faint squeal of tires.

"No, it's fine, really," she said. "If it's not too much trouble for you."

"No problem. Are you all ready for your class this morning?"

She laughed. "If I can only manage to find it this time, the rest should be easy! But," she continued more seriously, "to tell you the truth, I'm not at all ready. I don't really know what I'm doing. This is all so new to me."

He glanced over at her, then returned his eyes to the road. "You shouldn't be so down on yourself. You're already getting a good reputation at Garfield House, after just that one class."

"I am?"

"Yeah. I go there on Wednesday evenings, too, after I finish work. More kids wanted to take my class than I could handle in one session, so Tony asked me to do another one in the middle of the week. Don't be surprised if you get asked to do the same thing. I've already heard a few complaints from kids who can't get into your Saturday class or who are already committed to something else at that time."

Pamela digested this in silence. What would she say if Brenda or Tony did ask her to give more time? Her first impulse was to refuse. She didn't have time enough for her own work even now. She couldn't afford to give up more. On the other hand, by teaching the class, she could learn things about painting that she might not have discovered otherwise.

She left the question unresolved and returned to something Matt had said. "After you finish work," she repeated. "Do you have a regular job?"

"Yeah. My uncle owns a service station over near the Mill Creek Shopping Center. I work for him some afternoons and weekends. I'll be going over there this afternoon."

She had thought when she got in the car that his khaki pants and shirt were part of a popular new fashion trend. Now she noticed that the shirt had *Matt* embroidered in red over the left pocket.

"That must be hard on you."

"Not really," he shrugged. "I like giving the class, and I like working at the station, especially when I get to do something more than pump gas."

"Have you always liked cars so much?"

"For a long time. Of course, having my uncle around helped. He's always encouraged me. He gave me this car for my fourteenth birthday."

"Fourteen," she gasped. "What could you do with a car at fourteen? You couldn't drive it, could you?"

He laughed. "Not this baby I couldn't, that's for sure. Especially since the previous owner had bent it around a bridge abutment over on the interstate. I've spent more than two years putting it back together."

He reached out a hand and patted the top of the dashboard. "I'm just about done, too. After a paint job and a little work on the interior, she'll be as good as new. Maybe even better than new — I've worked pretty hard on her."

Pamela looked at him with new eyes. She didn't understand how someone could get so involved with a piece of machinery, but she knew how hard it was to devote yourself to a goal that might take a long time to achieve. She wanted that ability for herself, and admired it in others.

"What will you do when it's finished?"

"Hmm? Oh, I don't know — drive it awhile, then sell it and buy another junker, I guess. It's the challenge as much as anything. It's such a kick when you finally get something you've been working on to operate the way it's supposed to."

"I know what you mean."

"You do?" he said skeptically.

"Of course I do." She heard the defensive note in her voice and tried to explain more calmly. "Painting is one challenge after another. You don't often get everything to go right — at least I don't — but when I do, it's wonderful."

He glanced over at her. "Maybe you do understand," he said thoughtfully. He steered over to the curb. "Here we are — Garfield House. And they saved me a parking space this time."

As Pamela walked in the door, someone called her name. She looked around, expecting to see Brenda. Instead, Gloria Macmillan was bearing down on her with a big smile on her face. She smiled back.

"You're working here, too," Gloria exclaimed. "Isn't this a *marvelous* program? It's such a privilege to be able to help out." She looked over Pamela's shoulder and her eyes widened slightly.

"Oh, hello," she said to Matt. "I met you with Jonathan the other day, didn't I? I'm Gloria Macmillan. Oh, yeah, I remember, he mentioned that you were a volunteer here. It's a great place, isn't it?"

Matt nodded to Gloria but didn't respond to her question. To cover the awkwardness, Pamela said, "Gloria is on the art show committee with me."

"Great," Matt said coolly. "I have to get to my class. See you later, Pamela."

"What a hunk," Gloria said while Matt was still within earshot. "Do you know him well? What sort of class is he giving?"

"Auto mechanics," Pamela replied cautiously, "and I just met him a few days ago. But how about you? I didn't know you were a volunteer here. Have you been doing it long?"

"Oh, not very long really."

"This is just my second time. I'm still finding it a little confusing."

"Don't worry, that will pass. I'm sorry to rush off, but — "

"That's okay, Gloria. I'm running late, too. See you later."

Pamela looked around the room. Richie was biting his lower lip and scowling down at his pad. Dinah was staring dreamily into space. Steve, who looked no older than twelve, had his head bent over so low that his nose nearly touched the paper. Sarah was sitting perfectly still, feet and knees together, back straight. Only her right arm moved. And the fifth student, Carla, was scribbling furiously, as if the object was to cover the page with pencil lines.

All of them turned at the tap on the door. "I'll get it," Pamela said. "Go on with the exercise."

Brenda was standing in the hall. "I hope I didn't interrupt anything," she said in a low voice.

"You didn't. I asked everybody to take the last fifteen minutes of class to draw somebody looking out a window. The point is to make the viewer feel what the person in the drawing is looking at without showing it."

"Wow, that sounds hard."

"It is. I'm doing it, too, and I'm having a rough time," Pamela said with a laugh. "But I think the kids will learn from it. There must be a lot of exercises I could do with them. On Monday after school I'm going to the library to see if I can find any books on teaching art."

"That's great," Brenda said. "Sounds like you're getting really involved with the class. Which reminds me," Brenda continued. "I was talking to Tony about your class, and he's very impressed. Dinah and Richie both told him how much they enjoyed it, and lots of other kids seem to be interested, too."

"Brenda, I — "

"I know, I know. This class is already as big as you can handle. I realize that, and I wouldn't dream of asking you to take more kids into it. But here's what I was thinking. In a week or two, after we have a really good idea of how this one is going, maybe we could schedule a second class for sometime in the middle of the week. I would make sure that you got rides both ways, and the class would only be an hour long."

Pamela opened her mouth to refuse, but Brenda held up her hand. "No, don't answer now. Take some time, think it over."

"I'll let you know," Pamela began, "but I can tell you — "

She broke off. From somewhere nearby came the sound of someone screaming, a high-pitched noise almost like a steam whistle that went on and on without a pause for breath. She exchanged a quick glance with Brenda, who had suddenly turned very pale. Behind her, the door to her classroom was crowded with frightened faces.

"Stay there," she said. "We'll see what's wrong."

Brenda ran ahead of her to the stairs. Over her shoulder she saw a thin girl in a black dress standing in the center of the hallway. Her mouth was wide open, and her eyes were as blank as shuttered windows.

Brenda ran to the girl, grabbed her wrists, and said in a calm, soothing voice, "It's all right, Tina, it's all right."

Pamela edged closer, wondering how to help. From the far end of the hall, Tony was rushing toward them. Matt was right behind them.

With breathtaking swiftness the girl slipped out of Brenda's arms and rushed at Pamela. She had just enough time to put up her arms to protect herself. "Why did you do it?" the girl screamed, hitting Pamela with clenched fists. "I hate you! *I hate you!*"

She tried to back away out of reach, but the

girl followed, red-faced and screaming, a figure from a nightmare. Then Pamela's foot caught on the edge of a small rug and she felt herself toppling backward. She flung out her arms to keep from falling, and the enraged girl continued to try and hit her.

Then, as suddenly as it had begun, it ended. Someone caught Pamela, kept her from hitting the floor, and someone else was holding her attacker in a gentle but inescapable grip. Pamela closed her eyes and took a deep breath, then let it out slowly. Gradually, her heart stopped trying to pound its way out of her chest, and her pulse no longer roared in her ears. She opened her eyes and looked around.

Tony had his arms wrapped firmly around Tina and was whispering in her ear. She had stopped screaming and was beginning to weep. Pamela tried to get up, then realized that she was half sitting on the floor, supported by the strong arm of someone behind her. She knew even before she looked that it was Matt Jacobs.

"Pamela, are you okay? Are you hurt?" Brenda was trembling.

"No, I'm — " She turned her head to look at Matt and tried to smile. "I'm okay, really I am. I've taken worse spills playing field hockey."

"Come on," Matt said, lifting her to her feet. "I'll drive you home."

"But what about my class — "

"Don't be silly," Brenda said. "They'll be there next week. You ought to go home."

She knew they were right. She didn't feel centered enough to finish her class now, and after this uproar her students were not going to be in the right frame of mind to learn, either. They'd finish the exercise next week.

Matt pulled up in front of her house and switched off the engine. Pamela looked blankly out the windshield and tried to gather up enough energy to open the door.

"Are you sure you're all right?" Matt asked.

"I'm fine. Just a little shaken up, that's all."

"You must have been really scared," Matt went on. "I was."

"It was pretty scary," Pamela said. Suddenly, all the fear and tension she'd been holding back came to the surface. She could feel tears forming in her eyes and she blinked them back. She didn't want to cry in front of Matt. "I don't know that girl," she said in a quivering voice. "I never saw her before in my life. And she looked ready to *kill* me."

Matt nodded soberly. "I know. Sometimes things don't make any sense at all." Matt reached over and put his hand on her shoulder. Then he trailed his fingers along the curve of her neck.

Pamela was hardly conscious of Matt's touch.

"She must have been going through something really terrible to act that way, but I didn't feel sorry for her at all, just scared and furious."

"I'm not surprised. I sure didn't feel sorry for her. If they hadn't dragged her off you when they did, I would have punched her out."

"Matt!" she gasped.

"In an emergency you can't always stop to be polite."

Suddenly Pamela began to shiver. The harder she tried to stop, the worse it got. His hand slid from her shoulder to around her back and he drew her toward him and held her close. His warmth melted the ice that had kept her from crying. She pressed her face against his starched khaki shirt and let the tears come.

"Hey, it's okay," he murmured in her ear. "It's over. You're all right now. You have people all around who care about you. Nothing's going to happen to you."

Gradually her sobbing eased. She became aware that Matt was stroking her back and kissing her hair. When she raised her head to look at him, he kissed her forehead, her tear-filled eyes, her cheeks, her nose. Then, as if suddenly startled by his own actions, he pulled back and looked at her with solemn eyes. "I'm sorry, I didn't mean — "

Before he could finish, Pamela closed her eyes and pulled his head down until his lips met hers. His lips were warm and soft, as she had known they would be. She longed to stay wrapped in his strong arms. It felt so safe. The image of his rugged, sensitive face was beginning to erase the memory of Tina's contorted features. The emotion clutching at her heart was no longer terror, but it made her heart beat just as strongly.

Suddenly a derisive honk from a passing car reminded her where she was.

She straightened up. "I'd better go," she said softly.

"Yes, I guess so," Matt said. "I'll see you in school." But his arms, as if they were obeying a different authority, remained tightly around her.

"Matt? Can you come to a party at my house on Friday night?" She had almost forgotten to ask.

"Friday night? I think so, unless my uncle wants me to work late. I can probably get off in time, though."

"Great. I'd better go," she repeated.

"Uh-huh." This time he took his arms from around her, but as she reached for the door handle, he reached over and ran his fingers through her silky hair, then kissed her again, so swiftly and softly she thought she might have imagined it. A moment later she was standing on the sidewalk, watching the red and yellow Camaro disappear around the corner. She shook her head in wonder and confusion and started up the driveway to her house.

# *Chapter*
# *8*

Pamela prowled restlessly around the living room. She stopped at the couch to rearrange the cushions. Then she went to the window and tugged at the hand-printed cotton curtains. In between, she straightened all of the paintings and prints along the walls. She sat down on an armchair in the shape of a baseball mitt and studied the bronze coffee table with its maze of letters, numbers, and symbols cast into its top. That table had fascinated her when she was a kid, and she thought staring at its patterns now would calm her nerves. But she couldn't sit still.

She walked to the neon-framed mirror near the front door and stopped to peer at her reflection. Her hair was fluffy from that afternoon's shampoo. She patted it fretfully, wishing that it would stay where she wanted it. She had tried on three or four outfits before settling on a pair of blue stirrup pants and an oversized blue and black-striped sweater. Now, looking at herself again, she wondered if she should have worn her black pants and peach sweater. She sighed and turned away from the mirror. It was too late now. The kids would start arriving soon.

She took another quick survey of the living room and checked her mental list. The pretzels, nuts, and raisins were already out in the living room. She had mini-pizzas on a cookie sheet in the fridge, ready for the oven, and bottles of soda and juice chilling. A big jug of cider waited next to the stove, along with cinnamon sticks and cloves for mulling. She even had three flavors of ice cream in the freezer, though this was hardly the season for it.

Was there anything she had forgotten? She hadn't given a party in so long, not since her yearly birthday parties back in grade school, and her mother had taken care of everything then. She still didn't know where she had found the nerve to do this, and as the time drew closer she began to worry that no one would show up, leaving her alone with two dozen mini-pizzas to eat.

She put an old Aretha Franklin album on the stereo, then sat down on the couch and stared out the window at the dark, empty street. She was half listening for the rumble of an old Camaro. Would Matt be able to come? She had barely seen him in school all week. Of course, she wanted to get to know Brenda and Jonathan and Phoebe and Woody better, but it wasn't the same. She wanted him there most of all.

But if he came, how would he act? She hadn't talked to him since that awful day when he had

71

been so comforting, that day that they had kissed and she had wanted it to go on forever. Would it be awkward now? On Monday she had seen him in the hall after math class and hurried over to say hi. He had smiled and said hello, but he had seemed nervous, ill at ease, and he had hurried off to class at least two minutes sooner than he needed to. Twice more she saw him in the cafeteria with Gloria and she had waved, but hadn't gone over to talk to them.

The next time she saw him, he was deep in conversation with Jonathan Preston. She stopped and joined them, and Jonathan included her in the conversation, while Matt acted almost as if she weren't there at all. After a minute or so, she made some excuse and escaped, her cheeks blazing with shame and rage, determined to forget about him. Her determination lasted only an hour or so, until she passed him in the hall and he gave her a smile so sweet, so warm that her heart flipped over in her chest.

What was it all about? The only explanation she could think of was that he was warning her not to misinterpret their kiss, not to think it meant more than it did.

What had it meant really? Sometimes she was sure that there was a special connection between them, but other times she thought she must be fooling herself. Matt was such a kind, understanding guy. Wouldn't he have been just as nice, just as comforting, to anyone who had been through what she had? If she tried to pretend that it meant more than that, she might just end up embarrassing him and making herself miserable. She forced herself to think of something else and suddenly remembered she had left Angie in the backyard. She walked to the kitchen to open the back door and let her back in.

When she got back to the living room, a car — not the Camaro — pulled up and three people climbed out. Pamela swallowed a couple of times and straightened her sweater. It looked as though she was going to have someone to help her eat those pizzas after all.

"Hi, Pamela," Brenda said when she opened the front door. "I convinced Jonathan and Fiona to give me a ride over. Are we the first?"

She came in, followed by Jonathan and his English girl friend, whom Pamela scarcely knew. Brenda stopped just inside the living room and said, "I was just telling these guys how talented you are. Are any of these paintings yours?" She gestured toward the walls.

Pamela blushed. "Only that one." She pointed to a child's crayon sketch in broad strokes of red and blue that slightly resembled a house and a cow. "My mom framed it when I was about five, and she refuses to take it down."

Brenda made an elaborate show of examining it. "Hmm," she said. "I'd say it has great promise, wouldn't you, Jonathan?"

"Sure," he said, playing along with her. "Great colors. I've always liked red and blue for cows."

"He's very patriotic," Fiona explained crisply. When Pamela looked blank, she added, "Red, blue, and white, you know."

"That's red, white, and blue," Jonathan said with a laugh.

73

"I hardly see that there's any great difference. Do you, Pamela?"

"Well. . . ." She glanced down at her sweater. "It's an expression, that's all. The same way my sweater is blue and black, but bruises are always black and blue."

Brenda continued around the room, looking at the artwork. "I really like this," she said, stopping in front of a lithograph of a desert scene. "There's so much feeling in it. Who did it?"

Just then the doorbell rang and Pamela went to let in more guests.

Woody walked in with his girl friend Kim, followed by Phoebe and Michael. As Pamela was saying hello to them, she heard a familiar rumble from down the block. Her breath came a little faster, and she kept looking out the door over Phoebe's shoulder while Woody told some complicated story about a delivery they had just made for Earthly Delights, Kim's mother's catering service. The smile on Pamela's face broadened as Matt's form appeared at the foot of the walk. But quickly it faded. He wasn't alone. Even in the dim light she knew who it was just behind him.

She pasted the smile back on her face and called, "Hi, Gloria. Hi, Matt. Come on in."

Matt seemed embarrassed and almost reluctant to enter the house. "Um, sorry we're late, but Gloria needed a ride," he muttered. He followed her into the living room and stopped to stare at the baseball mitt chair. Woody, who had plopped himself down in it the moment he arrived, grinned up at him.

"I was caught on the rebound," he said.

When conversation started to pick up among her friends, Pamela went into the kitchen to get the cold sodas and prepare the hot cider. Little Angie clicked across the tile floor behind her and began nosing under the refrigerator for stray peanuts. On the top shelf of one of the cupboards Pamela noticed a wide cylinder of clear plastic, about a foot high. She vaguely remembered her mother using it for an arrangement of dried flowers years before. She found the stepladder, took down the cylinder, rinsed it out, and began to pour ice cubes into it. It might not have been designed as a soda cooler, but she couldn't think of any reason it wouldn't work as one.

"Can I do anything to help?" Brenda walked in through the swinging double doors.

Pamela looked up. "Sure, thanks, Brenda. You could bring me a few of the bottles from the fridge. I want to take out the soda, then heat up some apple cider."

"Yum. Great idea. This'll probably be our last chance this winter to have any. It's already starting to get warm."

Brenda brought three big bottles over and set them in the ice, then put her hand on Pamela's shoulder. "You know," she said, "I really admired how you reacted to the horrible scene at Garfield House last weekend."

"Well, there wasn't a whole lot I could do, was there?" Pamela said with a shrug. "Do things like that happen there often?"

"No, not often at all. That was a pretty rare incident. It was really scary. I couldn't believe how calm you were."

75

"Well, if you want to know the truth, I let it out afterward. I was pretty shaken up by the time I got home." Pamela shivered, remembering the scene in the car with Matt. She shook her head to clear her thoughts before her mind had a chance to visualize the kiss again.

"Well, now that you've had two bad experiences there," Brenda went on, "I hope it won't keep you from coming back again. It was rotten luck you've had. I don't know what I'd think of Garfield House if I were you."

"Don't worry about it, Brenda. I'm not thinking of quitting now. I'm anxious to see how the kids did with that exercise I told you about. Now, if something bad happens next time, I can't promise I won't change my mind," she finished up with a laugh.

Just then Fiona appeared at the kitchen door and scrunched up her face. "Do either of you know of some very engaging group activity we could introduce? I'm afraid Matt and Jonathan have begun to talk about cars. Unless we do something quickly, they may be at it for the rest of the evening."

"How about charades?" Brenda said, half seriously.

"Brenda, you're a genius!" Fiona exclaimed. "I haven't done that for an awfully long time. I do hope the rules are the same over here — I should hate to make a fool of myself."

"You'll probably make fools of *us*," Brenda replied. "I don't know about the others, but I'm not really in practice. I think the last time I played, my team acted out *The Cat in the Hat*."

Noticing Fiona's blank face, she added, "That's a favorite book in first grade here."

"Oh, I see." The petite English girl looked around the kitchen. "Is there anything I can carry out, Pamela?"

"Oh, no," she said quickly. She had been so lost in her own thoughts, she was startled by Fiona's question. Then she said suddenly, "Have Matt and Gloria known each other for a long time?" As soon as the words were out of her mouth, she remembered that they had just met once before the first time Gloria showed up at Garfield House.

"I hardly think so," Fiona said. "I'm sure Matt would have mentioned her before now if they had."

"None of us really knows Gloria very well," Brenda added.

If that was the case, how did she always manage to show up at all the crowd's activities? Pamela decided not to pursue the question further just now. Her other guests were out in the living room with nothing to drink and only raisins, nuts, and pretzels to eat. She picked up the cooler, which was surprisingly heavy, and started toward the door. She glanced back at Brenda. "Could you grab the cups, Bren? They're right behind you on the counter. And be careful not to step on Angie — she's really underfoot in this small kitchen."

Brenda grabbed the cups and napkins and went ahead. As they entered the living room, Matt saw Pamela staggering under the weight of the cooler and hurried over. "Let me help," he said, taking the outer edge of the cooler. The unexpected change in weight distribution threw Pamela off balance. Ice cubes skittered over the edge of the plastic cylinder and clattered onto the floor. Some quick footwork saved her from falling, but the cooler tipped the other way when she let go completely and ice and frigid water spilled down Matt's front and splashed down on Pamela's dog. Matt thrust the cooler back into her hands and jnmped back in surprise; Angie yipped and retreated to a corner in the kitchen.

Pamela didn't dare move. Her grip on the slippery smooth plastic was not that secure, and she couldn't see enough of the floor to keep from stepping on an ice cube. "Here," Matt said. His face was bright red. He slipped his hands under the cooler and took the weight of it from her. For a long, long moment his fingertips touched hers. Pamela thought all the ice would melt with the heat that shot through her from Matt's brief touch. Then he stepped back and carried his awkward burden to the table.

Pamela was mortified by her clumsiness. She knelt down to pick up the ice cubes, hoping the others couldn't see her blushing.

"Poor Matt," Gloria cooed. "You're all wet."

Pamela looked up from the floor and over at them. Gloria was trying to blot the water from Matt's shirt, and he was trying to get her to stop. Suddenly a painful expression took over his face. He finally managed to get Gloria to stop wiping at his chest. He stepped back, reached into his shirt pocket, and pulled out an ice cube. Everyone burst into laughter, and Woody led a round of applause. "What's next?" he called. "A rabbit?"

"No," Pamela said, straightening up. "A towel and a dry shirt. You guys help yourselves to soda. We'll be right back."

"I guess this little fellow could use a toweling off, too," Matt added. He picked up Angie, who was trying to shake herself dry, and obediently followed Pamela up the stairs. Gloria looked as if she wanted to come along but didn't quite dare. The sight gave Pamela a lot of satisfaction, but also left her feeling a little ashamed of herself.

"Here," she said, turning on the bathroom light and handing him a towel. She studied his shoulders and chest for a moment. "I'll get one of Dad's shirts. It may be a little small for you but it'll have to do."

"Hey, you don't need to — "

She closed the bathroom door on his protest. Her father had half a dozen cotton polo shirts in his drawer. She thought for a minute about Matt's coloring, selected a navy one, and returned to tap on the door. Matt opened it. He was holding the towel in one hand and wearing only his jeans. Wordlessly she handed him the shirt and fled, red-faced, down the stairs to find Gloria watching her with narrowed eyes.

It was just after twelve when Woody and Kim left. Pamela's dad was already home, up in his room reading. Brenda had offered to stay and help her clean up, and Matt had offered to help, too, then give Brenda a ride home. Gloria hadn't said anything. She was sitting at one end of the couch now, leafing through a magazine.

Pamela carried a bunch of dirty cups to the

kitchen and helped Matt put the plastic cooler back on its shelf. Her breath caught when their hands touched. When Matt climbed down from the stepladder, they found themselves eye-to-eye in the middle of the kitchen floor. Matt was just starting to reach around her when they heard Brenda call from the living room, "Hey, Pamela. Did you ever tell me who the artist of this is?"

Matt followed Pamela back to the living room where they found Brenda standing before the lithograph of a desert scene she'd asked about earlier in the evening.

Pamela took a deep breath. "No, I didn't tell you. My mom did that."

"She did? I really love it. It must be New Mexico, then." She looked at it for a few moments longer, shook her head admiringly, and turned away to take a stack of dirty plates to the kitchen.

"Has your mother spent a lot of time in the Southwest?" Gloria asked.

"Yes, she has," Pamela said, as casually as she could manage. "She lives there part of the year. She has a cabin in New Mexico, about ten miles from Taos."

"Really? My grandmother lives in Scottsdale. That's in Arizona."

Gloria picked up her magazine again, and Pamela sighed with relief. She didn't always understand her mother's way of life, but she was proud of her, and she didn't enjoy trying to defend her lifestyle to those with more conventional families.

Matt was leaning over to study the lithograph. "How is this kind of thing done?" he asked.

"It's pretty complicated," Pamela replied. "You

use a special kind of crayon to draw on a special kind of stone, then you ink the stone with a roller and press the paper down on it. The ink only sticks to the parts of the stone you didn't draw on, so when you pull the paper off it has the image printed on it."

"Neat," he said. "Whoever invented that had brains."

Brenda had turned from the kitchen. "That picture really makes me want to see New Mexico," she said. "What's it like there?"

Pamela wrinkled her brow. "Well — it's really hot in the summer and it gets pretty cold in the winter, but the sky is so big and open that you can't believe it. And the colors in the rocks are amazing. There isn't much green around, though."

"I don't know if I'd like that part of it," Brenda said. "Not for very long, anyway. Come on, guys," she said, looking at Matt and Gloria. "Let's finish straightening up and let Pamela get to bed. I'm already pushing my curfew."

They carried the last few things into the kitchen and put on their coats to leave. Matt gave her a quick peck on the cheek at the door. Ten minutes later, as she was drifting off to sleep, Pamela saw Matt's face when she closed her eyes, now funny, now tender, now serious and thoughtful. She sighed and rolled over to hug her pillow, content in the knowledge that she would see him again in the morning when he came to take her to Garfield House.

# Chapter 9

Peter glanced up and down the street, then led Monica into a dark, narrow alley. A few steps along, she stopped and looked back longingly at the street. It may have been dingy and depressing, but at least it had been well-lit.

"Are you sure this is the way?" she asked.

"Well — " he said doubtfully, then his tone changed. "Of course I am. That's the place right there."

The building he was pointing to looked as if it might once have been a stable. As they drew closer to the tall double doors, she saw a brass plate mounted on the front wall to the left of the doors. In the gloom she could just make out the words ELECTRIC MOMMA STUDIOS. Peter hunted around until he found a bell to push.

As they waited for someone to answer the door, Peter said. "This place has a real reputation — all the latest equipment, and engineers who know how to use it. I'm surprised Brent and the guys could afford to buy time here, especially on a Friday evening. Maybe they know someone."

From a concealed speaker somewhere over their heads a voice said, "Yes?"

Monica recovered first. "It's Monica Ford and Peter Lacey, from WKND. The Dial-Tones invited us to sit in on their session."

The voice didn't reply, but a moment later the door buzzer sounded. Peter grabbed the knob and tugged, then pushed. The door swung open and admitted them to what looked like a luxurious cave. The floors, the walls, and even the ceiling were covered in gray industrial carpeting over heavy padding. Hidden fixtures made pools of light around a tall climbing plant, an abstract sculpture, and a display case that contained four gold records and a dozen or more trophies and plaques.

"Studio B, downstairs," the voice said.

The atmosphere changed abruptly at the foot of the stairs. The floor was still thickly carpeted, but the walls were bare concrete blocks and the bulbs dangled nakedly from the high ceiling. A cardboard arrow taped to the wall bore the hand-lettered message STUDIOS B & C. When they followed in the direction it pointed, they found themselves in a narrow dead-end hallway. The door at the end was labeled CONTROL B/C. On the left was a door that said STUDIO B and on the right one labeled STUDIO C.

"Do we want the studio or the control room?"

Monica whispered. She wasn't sure why she was whispering. She had a feeling that she could shout her loudest without making any noise.

"The red light isn't on over the door to the studio," Peter whispered back. "We might as well try it."

The door opened when he pushed it. Monica followed him through and found herself standing on a gridwork balcony ten feet above the floor. A steel stairway led down to a scene of complete confusion. After a couple of minutes she managed to spot three of the members of the Dial-Tones, and at least five other people just wandering around. Heavy-duty electric cords crisscrossed the floor in every direction, held in place by lengths of silvery gaffers' tape. As she watched, two men wheeled an eight-foot-high partition out from somewhere and placed it between the drums and the speaker for the bass guitar.

"I'm glad you made it," Brent said from just behind them. He stepped between them and put one hand on each of their shoulders. "Quite a scene, isn't it?"

"It sure is," Peter said. "I wish I could figure out what everybody is doing down there."

Brent laughed. "So do I, my man, so do I. All I know is that the Beatles cut their whole first album in a little less time than it's going to take us to record one song. Of course they were using a two-track tape recorder, and ours has sixty-four tracks, so everything takes thirty-two times as long to set up. I wonder if our results will be thirty-two times as good."

Peter and Monica both laughed at this, although Monica half suspected Brent was serious.

She continued to scan the scene below them. "I don't see your keyboards anywhere," she said to Brent. "Aren't you playing tonight?"

"Sure I am. Recording engineers think singers are very dangerous creatures. You see that glass booth over to the right? That's where I go when we tape. When I close the door I can't hear a thing that's going on out here. It's a weird sensation, like suddenly going deaf."

"Wow, you mean you have to follow the whole thing through headphones?" Peter asked.

Brent nodded. "It takes getting used to, but so does hearing yourself over a stage monitor." He looked around as someone on the floor called his name. "I think they want me now," he said, giving Monica's shoulder a squeeze. "Why don't you stay up here or go up to the control room, whatever you like. Don't worry about being in the way, somebody'll tell you if you are." He half slid down the steep staircase and gave them a wave from the bottom.

"Isn't he terrific?" Peter said, before Brent was quite out of earshot. "And did you see how cool he is? How many guys do you think could be that on top of everything right before their first recording session? I'd be a wreck."

Monica wasn't sure whether it was his praise of Brent or his devaluation of himself that she found so irritating. "You've taped hundreds of hours and you've never been nervous. The biggest difference is that here you'd have someone else to worry about the engineering side of it."

He gave her a pitying look. "That's doing a

show," he said. "Any idiot with a big mouth can do that. I'm talking about performing, making music. It's a different thing altogether."

Monica was not in the mood for a fight so she didn't respond. She couldn't understand why Peter kept putting himself down every time they saw Brent. She turned away and watched the activity in the studio. One of the technicians was placing a whole battery of microphones around Zolly's drums, as if they were about to give a news conference. When he had them positioned the way he wanted, he began to snap his fingers next to one of them while looking up toward the control room window. After half a minute or so, he moved on to the next and snapped his fingers some more. Monica wondered if he had had to go through a finger-snapping audition to get his job.

If she had known exactly what all the technicians were doing, she might have found the scene fascinating. As it was, after about fifteen minutes of watching them, she grew bored. She thought Peter looked bored, too, but when she said something to him, he acted as though he were deeply involved, never taking his eyes off the activity below.

"Okay, gang," an amplified voice said, "let's clear the room and check some levels."

Zolly pushed himself up from the bench where he had been lounging and sat down behind his drums. Si and Roy strapped on their guitars and hunted around for their amp cords. Brent crossed the room, bowing to an imaginary audience, and climbed the steps to the isolation booth. In the doorway he turned and clasped both hands over his head, then shut the door and donned his head-phones.

"Can you hear me?" the voice said.

Through the window Brent gave a thumbs-up sign.

"We'd better beat it," Peter whispered. "I wonder if we can watch from the control room."

"Let's go see," Monica said. She led the way into the hall and tapped on the control room door, then opened it. A man in his thirties with a long moustache and a ponytail looked around, nodded, and returned his attention to the studio below.

"Bass," he said into a microphone that hung above the mixer panel, "give us a run from low to high." Roy nodded and started to play, but no sound penetrated the control room. The engineer was studying his array of meters, but for Monica and Peter it was like a mime show. "Thank you, bass. Charlie, move the mike a little closer to the speaker, would you? Good."

He adjusted two of the potentiometers, then said, "Drums?" Zolly looked up toward the booth. "When I give you the signal, can you give me a set of triplets on the toms, some taps on the cymbals from soft to loud, and a good solid whomp on the bass? Okay, go." Another silent movie unreeled. The engineer frowned, fiddled with several knobs, and asked Zolly to do it again. It took another five minutes before he was satisfied. By then there were six or eight little strips of masking tape with cryptic symbols on different parts of the board.

Before going on to Si, the engineer glanced around and seemed surprised to see Peter and Monica standing behind him. "Want to listen in?"

he said, pointing to a couple of headsets hanging from a hook. They grabbed them and put them on. As he continued to set the mike levels, Monica realized that she was becoming much more interested. The board was much too complicated for her to understand what was going on. The problem — balancing levels from different sound sources, isolating certain sounds, finding a distance at which a microphone yielded a real, unremote quality — were problems she confronted from time to time at the radio station. She thought she might even manage to learn something by watching the engineer solve his problems. She patted her pockets, but she hadn't thought to bring a notebook or even a piece of paper with her.

"Okay, fellows," the engineer said, leaning closer to his mike. "I'd like the opening of your first song now, all together. Take it through the first few bars of the vocal for me, please."

He sat back and scanned the banks of meters as the Dial-Tones strummed, drummed, and sang down in the studio. When they finished, he made tiny adjustments to several knobs and said, "Very nice. Why don't we break for five, then do a take."

He removed his headphones and swiveled his chair to face them. "You must be the kids from the radio station," he said. Though his tone was friendly, Monica sensed Peter bridling at being called a kid.

"That's right," she said quickly. "I'm Monica, and this is Peter."

"Hi, I'm Bob," he replied. "Any of this gear familiar to you?"

She nodded.

"Sort of," Peter said. "But this is a lot more sophisticated than anything I've used."

"Nah," Bob said. "A tape recorder's a tape recorder. The tape goes through and the sound goes on. All we really do that's different is lay down lots of tracks at one time, then mix them later. It's easier than trying to get everything exactly right in one take. Easier on us and a whole lot easier on the musicians."

He glanced over his shoulder at the studio. "Better get back to work," he said. "You guys hang out if you like. I'll give you a tour of the board next time we break."

"Great," Monica said as he swiveled back to face his controls. "Thanks."

"Yeah, thanks," Peter added, "but we're going to have to go pretty soon."

Monica looked at him in surprise. What was he talking about? She had freed up the whole evening for the recording session. Did he really mean to leave after only an hour or so?

"I'm sorry," he explained in a whisper. "I didn't know the session would go on so long. I promised to tape a concert tonight in Virginia. It's going to take me time to get there and time to set up."

"You never said anything about it to me."

"I'm sorry, I wasn't thinking." He reached out and took her hand. "Look, Monica, I know you wanted to watch the session. So did I. But I have to go, I promised."

"But I didn't promise, Peter," she said. "I'd really like to stay and watch."

"But how will you get home? This isn't the

greatest part of town, you know."

"I'll get one of the guys in the band to give me a ride," she said, "or else I'll take the bus."

"Well. . . ."

Monica was starting to get annoyed at his implication that she couldn't take care of herself. Peter looked at his watch. "Hey, I have to get going. I'm sorry, Monica. But, okay, if you're sure you want to stay. Be careful getting home. You can tell me all about the session tomorrow."

He leaned toward her, but she wasn't quite ready to kiss and make up. She turned her head away. He kissed her cheek, hesitated another moment, and left.

The closing door caught the attention of Bob, the engineer. He glanced around and saw that Monica was alone. Raising his eyebrows, he pointed toward an empty chair. "Thanks," she mouthed, putting on her headphones and sitting down at the board. He reached over and turned a knob in front of her, flooding her head with the sound of Brent and the band doing "Climb My Oak." They sounded terrific. She lowered the volume slightly and settled back to watch and listen.

They recorded four takes of "Climb My Oak," then moved on to the fast rocker that Peter had said was an imitation of "Gloria." After the third time through, Bob stood up and said into the mike, "that's dynamite, fellows. Somebody else is booked into the studio in half an hour. Why don't you come up here to the booth and we'll listen to a rough mix."

Si put his guitar down and stretched, then went over and clapped Zolly on the back. Roy joined them and they started up the stairs. Brent paused just outside his isolation booth to light a cigarette, then followed. They greeted Monica as they entered the control room, and Brent looked around.

"Where's my man Peter?"

Monica explained.

"Too bad," Brent said, but he didn't sound as though he meant it.

He came up behind her chair and put his hands on her shoulders. "You live in Rose Hill, don't you? If you want to hang around while we pack up, there's room for you in the van."

"Thanks. That would be great." She shifted uncomfortably. He took his hands away.

Bob made some adjustments to the board and said, "We can fiddle a lot with the final mix, but this will give you an idea."

He pushed a button. After a long, tense moment of silence, the opening bars of "Climb My Oak" came blasting out of the big speakers on the wall. By the end of the first verse, the guys in the band were grinning at each other and slapping hands.

Monica couldn't help grinning, too. She was thrilled to be there at that moment. The song might never make the charts, might never even be taken up and released by a recording company. But there was no question that it felt like a hit and that the band came off sounding like complete pros.

Bob played another take, then moved on to the second song. When it ended, Brent nodded thoughtfully. "It's solid," he said, "but definitely a 'B' side. Am I right?"

"Wait for the final mix," Bob advised, but Monica noticed that he didn't disagree.

Packing up the equipment didn't take very long. Brent helped load the van, then turned to Si. "How about you drive the van tonight and let me run Monica home in your car?"

"You got it, man," Si said. As he handed Brent the keys, he gave Monica a curious glance. She felt herself start to blush.

She followed Brent to a silver Honda where he unlocked the door and opened it for her. They drove in silence and before she knew it they were on the outskirts of Rose Hill. She gave him directions to her house, and a few minutes later he pulled up in front and shut off the engine.

"Thanks a lot," she said. "It was fantastic being able to watch your session like that."

"And thank you, Monica," he said softly. "Knowing you were up there in the control room made a big difference to me. I couldn't see you behind the glass, but I imagined you listening and moving to the music, and it gave it that extra edge. If our demo makes it, you deserve some of the credit."

"Oh, come on, Brent. I didn't have anything to do with it," she began, but his compliment made her glow inside. Before she knew what was happening, Brent reached out and pulled her toward him. She knew that she should back away, but somehow she couldn't make herself do it. As his lips pressed on hers, a shiver ran down her back. It was not just Brent she was kissing; he was a rock star. And when she wrapped her arms around him and moved closer, she was embracing the music she had loved for as long as she could remember. She was lost in it all.

Later, in her room, she sat on the edge of her bed and tried to understand what was happening to her. If she loved Peter, how could she respond so eagerly to someone else? Brent was not the kind of guy she wanted to get involved with, she knew that. Yet at the same time she felt herself drawn to him. There was definitely something magnetic about him. And the way Peter had been praising him up and down, making him out to be another Springsteen, it was almost as if he had been pushing her straight into Brent's arms. Was that his way of getting a closer connection with someone he admired so much? Monica felt incredibly confused. Up until now, she'd never doubted her love for Peter. She still didn't, really. But something strange was going on. And with the way Peter was acting around Brent, it was almost as if he was egging her on. Well, she thought, if anything *did* happen between her and Brent, Peter would have no one to blame but himself.

# Chapter
## 10

"Two emotions?" Dinah asked skeptically.

"That's right," Pamela said. "Two *different* emotions. You can be as realistic or as abstract as you like. But when you're done, write what emotion it is on the back, then cover it with tape. Next week we'll look at all of them and write down what emotion we think each one is related to, then compare our reactions to what the artist meant to communicate."

From the glances that went around the room, the kids were both excited about the assignment and scared by the thought of having all the others judging their work.

"What about you?" Steve asked. He had a sweet, boyish face, but Pamela found him sly and manipulative. "Are you going to do two drawings, too?"

"Of course," she said. "I'll take my chances and my knocks with the rest of you."

"All right!" Richie exclaimed. She wasn't sure if he was rooting for or against her.

"Okay, that's it," she said. "I'll see you all next Saturday. Have a good week."

As she gathered up her materials, she wondered where she was going to find the time to do her two sketches for the class. Between soliciting entries for the art show at school and preparing for her classes at Garfield House, she never seemed to have enough time to work quietly by herself. Had she made a mistake, agreeing to teach a second class? She had told Brenda this morning that she would take on another class if enough kids were still interested. She liked the kids and found them stimulating, and she liked the extra time with Matt, even though it never turned out quite like she hoped it would.

In the hallway she had to fight the urge to keep glancing over her shoulder. A full week had passed since the incident with Tina, but Pamela still felt shaken by it. Whenever anyone walked by her, she felt herself shying away as if they might leap at her unexpectedly. If someone were to sneak up behind her and say, "Boo!" she would probably jump right out of her skin.

Down the hall, Matt was just coming out of his classroom. Without meaning to, she walked more slowly, postponing the moment when she would have to say hi and talk to him. Their conversation on the way to Garfield House that morning had been awkward and uncomfortable, and the harder she tried, the worse it seemed to get. Matt just didn't seem to want to open up to her. Twice now she'd been in intimate situations with him, and each time afterward he acted as though nothing had happened. She was getting such mixed signals and she didn't know what to do about it.

She was a dozen feet from Matt now. She had to say something. "How was your class today?"

He glanced at her, glanced away, and shrugged uncomfortably. "All right, I guess."

"We had a good time in mine, talking about color and mood. What were you doing today?"

His discomfort increased visibly. "Ignition systems," he said. "Mostly distributors."

"Maybe I ought to take your class myself," she said with a smile. "Sounds like I could learn something."

"Um, well," he said, fidgeting. "I don't think you'd find it very interesting."

Pamela retreated into hurt silence. Did he think she was such a mechanical nincompoop that she couldn't handle his class? She'd never learned anything about cars, true, but she'd never had any reason to. Not until now.

"Are you ready to go?" he asked.

"Yeah." As soon as his back was turned, she angrily brushed the tears from her eyes. Why did she even bother caring about some boy who so obviously didn't care about her? She didn't need him. She could find another way to get back and forth to Garfield House.

"Hi, guys. How did it go this morning?"

"Fine," Pamela said. Gloria studied her for a moment, then turned her bright eyes on Matt. "How about you?"

"We had a pretty good time in my class," he

said. "We spent most of it talking about timing, adjusting an engine's ignition system so that the spark comes at just the right instant for best performance."

"It sounds very tricky," Gloria said.

"Yeah, it is. But these guys pick things up quickly. Hey, are you guys up for a pizza? We could stop on the way back to Rose Hill. My treat, I got paid yesterday."

"Not me, thanks," Pamela said quickly. "I've got a killer headache." This was only partly untrue. If she had to listen to Matt enthusiastically explaining auto mechanics to Gloria for two more minutes — when he'd hardly said a word to her — she was going to develop several headaches, one on top of the other.

"But don't let me stop you," she added. "You can drop me off and go on to the pizza shop from there."

"Well," Gloria began to say, "if you're — "

Matt broke in. "Hey, I just remembered. I promised Jonathan I'd come over as soon as I got back to Rose Hill. He's having trouble with his fuel pump. We'll do pizza another time, okay? All three of us."

For a split second Gloria looked furious. Then she smiled. "That would be great," she said. "Another time." Pamela didn't say a word.


"Turn it over a few times."

*Rrrr, rrr, rrr,*

"Okay, hold it. That'll do it." Matt pulled his head out from under the hood and straightened up. He pulled a rag from his hip pocket and wiped his hands as he said, "You guessed it. It's the fuel pump all right."

Jonathan pushed himself up out of the driver's seat and swung his legs over the side of the car. He had been practicing that maneuver ever since getting the old convertible. Occasionally he forgot and tried to do it when the top was up. But that was very rare. Except on the coldest days, or during rain or snow, the top was down. When the temperature dropped, he simply wore a warmer coat.

"What about the one I got?" he asked Matt. "Do you think it'll fit?"

Matt went over to the workbench and picked up the reconditioned fuel pump. "Looks the same," he observed. "Yeah, it ought to fit. They don't change fuel pumps every year the way they do taillights. Anyway, we'll know in an hour or so, won't we?"

They put rubber mats on the fenders, to protect the finish, laid out the tools they thought they would need, then got to work. By now they had been working together so long that they hardly needed to talk. In less time than they expected, they had the faulty fuel pump disconnected and out of the car.

"Let's take a break," Jonathan said. "My fingers are a little numb from the cold. Let's go inside and I'll make a pot of tea."

Matt smiled. "Fiona's going to make an Englishman out of you yet."

"It's a two-way street, buddy. I've got her eating subs and hot dogs. Maybe we'll sort of meet halfway between England and the U.S."

"Like in Greenland, you mean?" Matt laughed. "I don't think you'll want to keep 'Big Pink's' top down *there*." He clapped Jonathan on the shoulder and the two of them went into the house.

Fiona had taught Jonathan the whole tea-making ritual. He filled the kettle with cold water and put it on the stove. While it was heating, he filled the teapot with hot water and let it sit until the kettle started to whistle. Then he emptied the water from the teapot, carefully measured in the loose tea, and took the teapot to the stove.

"Very important," he explained. "Always carry the tea to the water, not the water to the tea."

"Why?"

"Beats me. I think it's written in their constitution." He poured the boiling water into the pot, replaced the lid, and brought the teapot to the kitchen table. "Milk or lemon, Matt, old chap?"

His elaborate seriousness made Matt grin. "Which do you recommend, Sir Jon?"

"Milk. We don't have any lemons. And since we've known each other for so long, you don't have to use my title."

"Well, okay. Whatever you say." He held out his cup to be filled, added milk and sugar, and took a cautious sip. The ritual might have seemed silly, but he had to admit the tea was good. He took another sip, then held the cup in both hands.

After a short silence, Jonathan said, "Okay, Matt, spill it. What's eating you?"

Matt frowned and shrugged his shoulders, but didn't say anything.

Jonathan studied him shrewdly. He let a few

moments pass, then said, "I guess it'll be Twenty Questions then, huh? Okay, what about Pamela Green? She's nice, isn't she? Talented, too. I loved it when you two fought over the ice bucket last night."

Matt grunted and looked intently at the teapot.

Jonathan gulped his tea and put his cup down hard enough to make the spoon rattle in its saucer. "All right," he went on in an exasperated voice, "tell me to butt out if you want, but I sure hope you're not getting hooked up with Gloria Macmillan."

"Gloria's not so bad," Matt said, looking up.

"She's a real schemer," Jonathan said, shaking his head. "I still can't believe the way she conned her way onto the art show committee."

"You're all too down on her," Matt insisted. "But it doesn't matter. I'm not interested in her, if that's what you're afraid of."

"What I'm afraid of is that something's wrong with you, and you're not telling me what it is. I'm your best friend, right? So give."

Matt picked up his spoon and began to trace patterns on the tabletop. "It's not important," he said slowly. "I just wish I was more cultured, that's all."

"Like yogurt, you mean?" Jonathan said. Before Matt could reply, he continued, "Okay, okay, it's not funny. Now what are you talking about? Drinking tea and talking about the latest Jane Austen novel? There's your tea, and the library is only five blocks away."

Matt's face tightened. "That's not what I mean

at all. It's just — " He hesitated, then burst out, "Look at Pamela. She's an artist, a real artist. And her family — her father's an artist, her mother's an artist, her brother's an artist, and the dog's probably an artist, too! What am I? A grease monkey, that's all. I can't even talk to her. I don't have anything to say worth her listening to. This morning, when I was driving her and Gloria back to Rose Hill, the only thing I could think of to talk about was timing lights!"

"Was she interested?"

"How should I know? I couldn't see her face, she was in the backseat."

Jonathan reached across the table and grabbed his arm. "What kind of yo-yo are you?" he demanded. "If you care so much about what she thinks, what are you doing putting her in the backseat?"

"I don't put her in the backseat," he protested. "She likes to sit back there. She always gets in back and Gloria sits in front."

"Is that so?" Jonathan said, looking thoughtful. Then he shook his head. "Well, buddy, I think I see your problem."

"Terrific," Matt said despondently. "Now how about a solution?"

# Chapter
# 11

On Sunday afternoon the planning committee for the art show met at Jonathan's house. From upstairs came the faint sound of Mrs. Preston's clackety typewriter. They settled down around the kitchen table and Jonathan brought out a carton of milk and a plate of freshly baked muffins. Pamela looked at the muffins longingly. She had been working earlier and skipped lunch. She took one and accepted a glass of milk.

Dee gave the first report. "I spoke to Sasha, and she promised to give the show a big story on the front page next week," she said. "As a matter of fact, she assigned me to get a good photo to go with it. Any ideas you have, let me know."

She paused for a sip of milk, then continued. "As for WKND, Peter Lacey is going to do a lot of plugging on his show, and Karen Davis may interview one of us the day before the opening."

"Great work, Dee," Gloria said, reaching for a

muffin. "I'll be glad to do the interview if no one else wants to bother with it."

"Wait a minute. Why us?" Jonathan said, making a wide gesture with his hand. He forgot he was holding his six-year-old sister's toy airplane. It gave a loud *whirr* and nearly hit Pamela in the face. He looked at it in surprise and set it down on the table.

"Sorry, Pam," he said. "But what I mean is, all we're doing is organizing the show as a service to the school. Why doesn't Karen interview some of the students who'll be in the show and find out what it means to *them*."

"Good idea." Dee scribbled a note in her pad. "I'll suggest it to her tomorrow."

Gloria looked slightly cross.

"One more thing," Dee said. "Pamela has designed a super leaflet for the show. I went yesterday and had a bunch of them printed up. Tomorrow we should put them up around school in place of the one we did asking people to submit their artwork."

"Sounds good to me," Jonathan said. "Why don't we meet in the cafeteria during lunch." He looked around the table. Everybody nodded. "Okay. Next thing, as you all know, the show is scheduled to run from Tuesday through Friday, the third week of March. I originally asked the administration to give us the entire week, but that made for some problems about when to set it up."

"When *do* we set it up?" Gloria asked.

"What I was about to say is that we'll set up on Monday after school hours. Someone from maintenance will be hanging around until a little before nine, so we have about six hours."

"To do everything? That's pretty tight," Woody said.

"I know, but I think we can manage. If necessary, we can deal with some last minute details during first period on Tuesday. I hope we won't have to."

"Are we going to do everything ourselves, just the five of us?" Pamela asked.

"Looks that way. I think we can handle it, don't you?"

"Well . . . sure, I think we can, but I thought maybe I'd ask my dad to come by and take a look. He's a designer and he might have some good suggestions to make. That is, if it's okay with the rest of you."

"I thought this was supposed to be a student project," Gloria said.

"It's a show of student artwork, sure," Jonathan replied, "but I don't see any reason why we can't get outside help in setting it up. Personally, I'd welcome some professional advice. I've never done anything like this before."

"None of us has," Woody added.

"Sure, Pamela," Jonathan concluded, "I think it's a great idea. Now let's have your report. How are the submissions going?"

"Really well. So far about forty kids have submitted work for the show, and some of them have turned in more than one piece. That's more than I expected, anyway, and we still have over a week to go. I'm impressed with the level of the work, too. Some of the things are fantastic, and even the ones that aren't great are really good. I think the show is going to surprise people. There's more talent around Kennedy than anybody suspects."

"That's good to hear," Jonathan said. "Okay, let's see, what else do we have to — "

"I have a report to make," Gloria said.

"Okay, Gloria. Go ahead."

"Well — " She paused and looked around the table, as if to make sure they were all paying attention. "After our last meeting I tried to think of something I could do to help the project along. Then it came to me. All the kids in the show use art materials all the time, and probably a lot of the people who'll come to see the show do, too. So last Thursday I went over to Dellarbor's, the art supply store in the shopping center, and had a long talk with the manager. I finally got him to agree to donate gift certificates as prizes for the top five entries in the show. What do you think of that?" She crossed her arms and sat back with a smug expression on her face.

There was a short silence. Then Pamela said, "But Gloria, this is supposed to be a show, not a contest. There won't be any top five entries. They're all equal."

"What do you mean, all equal? Are you trying to tell me that none of the paintings is any better than any of the others? You just said yourself that some of them are fantastic. Don't they deserve recognition?"

"Sure they do. And they'll get it, too. People will walk by, stop, and realize that they're fantastic. That's recognition enough. But if we start giving out prizes, it's like saying the people who don't get them aren't any good."

"Well, if they were any good, they'd get a prize."

Woody intervened. "I think what Pamela means is that we set this up as a cooperative student art show. If we turn it into a competition instead, with winners and losers, it's like betraying what we set out to do."

"Well, I think a competition is the way to go! Do you expect me to go back to the man at Dellarbor's and tell him we won't take his donation? That's ridiculous!"

"That's a good point," Dee said. "It'd be like insulting him for trying to do a nice thing for Kennedy High."

Pamela pressed her thumb against the bridge of her nose and prayed that her impending headache would pass. She did not want to prolong the dispute with Gloria, but she couldn't let the art show be turned into a competition. "Isn't there some way we could have him do something for all the kids in the show?" she said.

"Like what?" Gloria said sarcastically. "Give each of them a gift certificate worth fifteen cents?"

"Of course not. But — " Why wouldn't her brain work when she needed it? "Look, we'll need some sort of program for the show, won't we? A list of the exhibitors and their works?"

"Sure," Woody said. "We didn't think of that."

"Well, why don't we ask Dellarbor's to pay the cost of printing up a really nice program? They could even run an ad on the back page. It would be really good business for the store."

She looked around the table. Jonathan was nodding slowly, Dee seemed to approve, and

Woody was grinning broadly. Only Gloria was frowning and giving Pamela a nasty look. The moment their eyes met, however, her expression changed. She flashed Pamela a rueful smile, as if to apologize for trying to make the art show into a cut-throat competition.

When the meeting broke up, Jonathan took Pamela aside. "I told Matt and Fiona I'd meet them at the sub shop after we finished here," he said casually. "Want to come along? We can get a sandwich, then maybe take in a movie together."

Pamela felt torn. A canvas was waiting on her easel at home. She'd already blocked in the major masses with weak ocher, and she was eager to start working with color. On the other hand, she liked both Jonathan and Fiona and wanted to get to know them better. This seemed like a perfect opportunity. As for Matt, he might act differently around his old friends than he did alone with her. And of course, her stomach reminded her, she *had* skipped lunch.

"Thanks, I'd love to," she said.

"I'm on my way," Woody called. "Anyone need a lift somewhere?"

"Would you mind dropping me at the library?" Dee asked. "I can walk home from there."

"A free trip to the library," Woody cracked. "Check it out! How about you, Gloria?"

"Oh, I don't think so," she said. "I was hoping to get a snack somewhere before I went home. Is anybody else interested?"

Pamela's heart sank. She exchanged a dismayed

glance with Jonathan, who hesitated a moment before saying, "We're going by the sub shop, Gloria. Do you want a ride?"

A flash of triumph crossed her face, and Pamela realized that she must have overheard Jonathan's invitation. "That would be great," she said. "I love convertibles."

Once more Pamela somehow found herself in the backseat. With the top down she couldn't even hear what Gloria and Jonathan were saying in the front. The cold March wind whipped around them and her nose and ears were getting numb. She zipped her parka up all the way, wrapped her scarf around her head and ears, and thrust her hands deep into her pockets, all the time wishing she had just asked Jonathan to take her home.

When they walked into the sub shop, Matt flashed her a huge smile, though he gave Jonathan a single reproachful look. Fiona, for some reason, greeted them all coolly. There was obviously something on her mind. She sat with her chair pushed back from the table and didn't speak to anyone. When Jonathan asked her if she wanted anything else from the counter, her answer was blunt and monotone. This definitely wasn't the same girl Pamela had chatted and traded jokes with at her party.

She wasn't really feeling very chatty herself. She ate her grilled cheese sandwich and potato chips and listened to Matt and Jonathan talk about the trouble they'd had getting parts for their cars. Twice Gloria tried to turn the conversation to people they knew at school, but the guys didn't seem to be in a gossipy frame of mind.

Pamela was nibbling moodily at a slice of pickle when Fiona sat up straighter, sniffed, and said in a clipped voice, "Jonathan, I don't feel very well. Would you mind taking me home?"

He looked surprised but said, "Uh, okay. We can go right now if you like."

"Yes, please."

"I ought to go, too," Pamela said quickly. "If it's not too far out of your way."

"Of course not," he said. He looked quizzically around the table.

"Oh, don't worry about me," Gloria said. "I'm going to have some dessert. Matt will take me home, won't you, Matt?"

Matt's cheeks turned pink. "Uh, sure," he said.

As she climbed into the backseat of the convertible, Pamela looked back through the misted windows of the sub shop. Matt was slumped in his chair with his hands clasped in front of him, staring down at the table, while Gloria carried on a vivacious, if one-sided, conversation.

# Chapter

# 12

Pamela was leaving school on Tuesday afternoon when she heard a familiar voice call her name. She groaned under her breath and turned around.

Gloria was hurrying down the steps toward her. "Hey, I'm glad I finally caught up with you," she said. "I've been wanting to talk to you ever since Sunday."

"About the art show?" Pamela asked.

"No, and not about the meeting, either." She linked her arm with Pamela's, and they continued to walk. "But about what happened afterward. I was pretty upset. I mean, Jonathan is such a sweet guy — isn't it a shame that he had to get involved with the winner of the Iceberg of the Year award? But maybe that's an example of the English reserve you always hear about."

"She wasn't *that* bad," Pamela said. "Something was just bothering her. I like Fiona."

"Oh, so do I! We're great friends. But you have to admit she was pretty cold on Sunday."

"Well. . . ."

"I'm afraid I'm the reason, too," Gloria continued in a lower voice. "That's what I wanted to talk to you about. I know I can trust you to keep a secret."

Pamela looked over in alarm. She did *not* want to be Gloria's confidante. But before she could protest, Gloria continued.

"You've probably noticed that Matt and I have been spending a lot of time together in the last few weeks." She looked at her with bright eyes. Pamela reluctantly nodded. How could she have failed to notice?

"I think that must be the reason that Fiona is so down on me," Gloria said. "You know, Matt is Jonathan's best friend, and I think she's been planning to get him hooked up with this other girl — one of *her* best friends. But I got in the way of her plan, and she doesn't like it."

Pamela frowned. Was this true? She didn't know if Fiona had plans to fix Matt up with any of her friends. She hadn't heard anything about it. On the other hand, Fiona had been upset with Gloria on Sunday afternoon, and she must have had a reason.

Gloria seemed to read her thoughts. "Of course there's more to it than that. Do you know her older brother Jeremy? When we first met, he made this *big* play for me. Well — what an Englishman thinks of as a big play, anyway." Her laugh had a harsh edge to it. "I thought he was very sweet and liked him a lot, but, you know, not that way. I let him know how I felt as nicely as I could, but he didn't like it at all. That was when he started dating Diana Einerson. And I guess Fiona still resents me for turning down her brother."

"I see," Pamela said faintly. She felt as if she had spent the school year walking blindly through an enormous room in which dozens of dramas were taking place — and she hadn't noticed any of them.

"But it's not Fiona I wanted to talk to you about," Gloria continued, lowering her voice again. "It's Matt. You see, well, Matt and I have a kind of special thing going on between us. You probably suspected that already. We haven't been very good at hiding how we feel. We've decided we have to do our best to seem like good friends and nothing more, and I want you to help us."

"I don't understand." She couldn't tell if she was more upset or confused by Gloria's revelation. "If you're seeing each other, why do you have to hide it? And why do you need my help to do it?"

"It's Garfield House. Didn't you know? They have a very strict rule against counselors and volunteers getting involved with the kids or with each other. We can thank our dear friend Brenda for that."

"What do you mean? Brenda doesn't make the rules there."

Gloria snickered. "She may not make them, but she seems to know how to bend them well enough. You must have heard people talking about it last year. She started spending time — a *lot* of time

— with one of the guys she was supposed to be counseling — some biker who was living at Garfield House."

"What happened? Were they caught?"

"They went out for a midnight ride on his motorcycle and had an accident. Brenda was hurt pretty badly. And the worst part is that the guy just rode off and left her there. No one's seen him since, not that anyone's looked very hard. Well, ever since then, the people who run Garfield House have been getting down on anyone who breaks the rule against fraternizing."

"So you and Matt — "

"If they find out, they'll throw us out. It's that simple. I don't know if I'd mind that much — who needs a place with a rule like that — but Matt is very involved with his teaching there. It would hurt him a lot to have to leave."

In her mind, Pamela saw Matt leaning over the table, face lit up, taking a carburetor apart while he explained to the eager kids exactly what each part did. Gloria was right — giving that up would be a real blow to him.

"That's why we have to keep our relationship a secret," Gloria continued. "It's really helped, having you with us all the time as a smokescreen. But I thought it was only fair to let you know what's going on. Please don't breathe a word to anyone, though, not even Matt. You never know who might accidentally overhear, and before you know it, the rumor will be all over the school. You won't say anything, will you?"

"No," Pamela said, shaking her head. "No, I won't say anything."

She stiffened as Gloria gave her an impulsive hug. "Oh thank you," Gloria exclaimed. "I knew I could count on you!"

The next day as she was leaving the cafeteria, she came face-to-face with Matt. She nodded and started past him, but he stopped her.

"Hey, I'm glad I ran into you," he said. "I'm going to be a little late picking you up this evening. I have to work an extra half hour at the service station. I didn't want you to worry."

"Oh." She suddenly realized that she could not stand another ride in the backseat of his car, acting as a chaperone for him and Gloria. "That's okay," she said, "I won't need a ride tonight."

"You won't?" He looked upset. Was he worried that someone else would see him and Gloria alone in the car and jump to conclusions? "Are you sure? It's no trouble for me to pick you up."

She shifted her eyes and tried to think of a reasonable excuse. She didn't want to tell him a lie, even though he hadn't been very honest with her. "I've been wanting to take a look around some of the art galleries in Georgetown," she improvised. As soon as she said it, she realized that it was true. "I haven't done that in months, and I really miss it. I'll take the bus in this afternoon, then get a sandwich somewhere before going to Garfield House."

"Well, okay then. I guess you need your regular doses of culture, don't you? I'll think of you while I'm scraping bugs off windshields and pumping gas." With that he turned and walked away.

Pamela stared after him with stinging eyes.

What Matt said wasn't unkind, but the *way* he said it was downright nasty. Indignation mixed with her pain. He had no right to treat her that way, just because she wouldn't go along with his and Gloria's scheme. She had thought he was a nice guy. She had even thought he liked her. And that kiss in the car. . . . Now it seemed she was wrong. Well, she thought, the less contact she had with a guy like that, the better.

But if she really believed that, why did she feel an empty, aching spot in the pit of her stomach?

When her class at Garfield House was over, Pamela went looking for Brenda. She found her in Tony's office, writing up a report.

Pamela was too concerned to bother with preliminaries. "Can you give me a ride home tonight?" she blurted out.

Brenda raised her eyebrows. "What about Matt? Can't he take you? I'm not quite ready to go yet."

"Oh, I don't mind waiting." She was on the point of saying something about Matt and Gloria. She stopped herself just in time.

"Okay," Brenda said, giving her a shrewd look. "Actually, I've been looking for a chance to talk to you, anyway. Just give me a few minutes to bring my journal up to date."

The wait turned out to be more like half an hour, but Pamela didn't mind. It was a stronger guarantee that Matt and Gloria were already out of the building and on their way home. She didn't want to have to make up another excuse for not riding with them.

In the car Brenda said, "I keep hearing great things about your class, Pamela. How would you feel about having a small exhibit of the kids' artwork at the end of the year? Do you think they'll be ready? Will they get anything from it?"

"Why . . . sure, they'll get a lot out of it. Art is about communication, passing on to someone else a particular way of seeing. It's very important to have an audience sometimes. You don't do all the creating just for yourself. I think it's a great idea."

"Well, I can't take any credit for it," Brenda said. "It was the art show at school that gave me the idea, and you were the one who thought of that. Will it be very much work to organize?"

"I don't think so," Pamela said. "There's lots of wall space in the hallways. Or we could put it up on the walls of the room where we have class. The kids will help."

"Great. I'll mention it to Tony the next time I see him, though I don't see why there should be any objection from anyone."

They drove a few blocks in silence. As they pulled up at the traffic light, Brenda cleared her throat. "Um, Pamela," she began, "there was something else I wanted to ask you. How do you think Gloria is working out as a volunteer?"

Pamela's eyes widened in confusion. Why was Brenda asking her? What on earth was she going to say? "Well, she's been working there a lot longer than I have, Brenda. I'm sure you know more about her work than I do."

"No. You both started at about the same time.

As a matter of fact, I think she started about a week after you did."

Pamela couldn't understand it. She was positive that Gloria had been at Garfield House for much longer than she had. She certainly acted like she knew everything about the place. Pamela still didn't know what to say about her to Brenda. Did she suspect that Gloria and Matt were more than friends? Was she hoping to get confirmation from Pamela? If so, she was going to be disappointed. Pamela wouldn't be able to live with the knowledge that she had helped get Matt kicked out of Garfield House.

On the other hand, Brenda might just want her opinion of Gloria's work. That raised problems, too. She had no idea what Gloria did at Garfield House. How could she possibly evaluate what kind of job she was doing? Occasionally, Pamela had seen her in conversation with some of the kids, but for the most part she seemed to do nothing but hang around Matt.

She couldn't possibly say that to Brenda, though. It would sound entirely too jealous and spiteful, and maybe it was. Maybe she was so soured by her disappointment at hearing Gloria was involved with Matt that she wasn't able to react to her objectively.

Suddenly Pamela was thoroughly sick of the whole business. Everywhere she looked was another twist, another complication. There was no painless way out, not for her. She should never have gotten involved with Matt, or Gloria, or Brenda, or any of them. She should have kept to herself, doing the work that she knew she loved. Instead, she had gotten herself into a game that she didn't understand, couldn't afford to play, and couldn't possibly win.

"Listen, Brenda," she began, "I can't keep this up."

"Keep what up? What do you mean?"

What *did* she mean? That she couldn't keep pretending to herself she didn't care for Matt Jacobs? Couldn't keep pushing the pain she felt into some far-off corner of her mind? She did mean that, but telling Brenda that wouldn't help. She could only see one way out of a situation that was becoming increasingly unbearable.

"I can't go on giving the classes. It's taking too much time away from my own work, and my marks are suffering."

"I can really sympathize with that," Brenda said. "But those kids have really come to rely on you. And they enjoy it so much. Maybe you could cut it back to just the Saturday class, but make it a bigger one. Would that work for you? It's such a worthwhile activity, Pamela. I'd hate to see you give it up so soon."

By concentrating very hard, Pamela was able to avoid sniffing, though the tears in her eyes were starting to sneak down her cheeks. At least it was dark in the car, so Brenda couldn't see her distress.

When Pamela didn't respond, Brenda went on, "Well, do you think you can find a way to keep going? Those kids need you."

"I know. And I do want to help. But it's too much, I can't take it."

"I understand."

Pamela couldn't stand the coldness in Brenda's voice. "I won't leave right away," she said. "Maybe I could. . . . What if I stay for two more months — that's enough, isn't it? And we can still have a show before I leave."

"If you can't do more, that'll have to do," Brenda said. "We can't ask for more than you can give."

In Pamela's ears the words sounded just like a slamming door.

Later, she sat in her bedroom by the window, gazing out into the night, her sketch pad balanced on her knees. The sky was not really dark; a curtain of clouds had moved in and reflected the distant lights of the city. As she thought and watched the changing sky, her hand and the charcoal it gripped moved over the surface of the pad almost with a will of its own.

When she realized how late it was, she stretched, wincing at the sharp prickles in her left foot, and started to stand up. Then she saw the sketch pad and froze. She really had been drawing without thinking. The building was more suggested than drawn, but it was unmistakably Garfield House, and the figure going up the front steps, turning to look over his shoulder, bore a definite resemblance to Matt Jacobs.

But that had not caused the chills that began at the base of her skull and traveled all the way down her spine. The background, which looked at first glance almost like trees or clouds, was in reality a shadowy face. It loomed larger than the building and boy combined, and its expression was both blank and menacing, as if caught in the middle of casting a spell.

Pamela stared in fascination at the sketch, then, with a decisive gesture, shut the book. She leaned her head against the wall and gazed at the window a moment longer. This only proved what she'd been trying so hard to deny to herself — Matt and Garfield House both meant something to her, and Gloria seemed to be trying awfully hard to threaten her relationships with both.

# Chapter
# 13

"I think we're in good shape," Jonathan said. Behind him was the usual confusion of the cafeteria at lunchtime, and from the speaker in the ceiling over his head came Peter Lacey's voice, introducing a song by yet another unknown band that might be destined for stardom. Pamela sometimes wondered how Peter found all the records he played. So many of them were rock groups neither she nor anyone she knew had ever heard of, and lots of them were very talented. She shook her head to bring her attention back to the committee meeting.

"There's one thing we haven't talked about," Jonathan continued, "and it's probably as important as any of the questions we've been dealing with. How are we going to make a really big splash on the day we open? We want every student at Kennedy to know about the show and to want to come see it."

"Free soda and peanuts, dancing girls, and a Clint Eastwood movie," Woody suggested.

"Really, Woody, it's not a laughing matter," Gloria said primly. "I agree with Jonathan. Publicity is very important, especially while the show is going on. I'd like to volunteer to be in charge of it."

The silence that greeted her announcement was brief but charged. Pamela glanced once at Gloria, then fastened her eyes on her notebook again. She had managed to avoid Gloria for almost a week, but she could not bring herself to drop out of the planning committee for the art show. It had been her idea in the first place, and she couldn't let it be ruined because she was too cowardly to attend a meeting. Once she was sitting across the table from Gloria, however, she found that she couldn't look at her. Instead she engrossed herself in drawing a series of cartoons based on famous paintings.

Jonathan broke the silence by saying, "Thanks, Gloria. We all know how efficient you can be when you take something over."

Pamela noticed Woody suppress a grin. Had Jonathan just made a subtle dig at Gloria?

"However," Jonathan continued, "I'm not sure that efficiency is what we need the most. What we want is an idea that has real flair."

Dee frowned in concentration. "How about balloons with a message printed on them?"

"Sure, the teachers would love that," Woody replied, "especially when everybody started popping them in class."

Jonathan said, "Right, no balloons. Any other ideas?"

"We could string a very long banner across a corner of the quad," Gloria offered.

"Sure," Woody said, "and if it started to sag in the middle, we could fasten Dee's balloons to it."

"Come on, you guys," Jonathan said. "Does anybody have any *good* ideas for how to promote the show?"

Woody nudged Pamela. "How about you?" he asked. Then he looked down at the cartoon she had been drawing. It was based on one of Picasso's Cubist paintings and showed a man whose head appeared to be facing in several directions at once. The caption under it said: WHICH WAY TO THE ART SHOW?

"That's terrific, Pamela," he said. "Hey, I wonder if there's some way we could use it."

"Use what?" Jonathan asked.

"Can I show them?"

Pamela nodded, and he held up the notebook for the others to see.

"I like it," Dee said, "but we already have the other poster Pamela did. What we need now is some way of catching the attention of the kids who never even look at bulletin boards. I don't think another poster will do it."

"Not a poster," Woody said. "A sandwich board."

"Say what?" Jonathan demanded.

"A sandwich board! You know, you wear it on your front and back, with straps over your shoulders. Pamela, do you think you could do this over on a big sheet of poster board?"

"Sure," she said.

"How about three or four others with different pictures but the same idea? Any problem?"

"Well. . . ." There were already two more cartoons in the notebook he was holding. One was a parody on Botticelli's "Birth of Venus," and the other a famous French painting from the 19th century called "Liberty Leading the Masses." In both, the point was how eager the characters were to get to the art show. "I think I could do that."

"Then there's our solution. We're in business!"

"Um, Woody," Jonathan said dryly, "I'm glad you've solved our problem, but do you think you might tell the rest of us exactly how?"

"Don't you get it?" Woody said excitedly. "I can see it now! It's next Tuesday — our opening day. Practically no one pays any attention. But then, during the break between first and second period, people appear in the hallways wearing sandwich boards. In front they have one of Pamela's cartoons, and in the back a big sign that says: FOLLOW ME TO THE ART SHOW. They appear after second period, too, and so on, and come lunchtime they stage a parade through the cafeteria. I guarantee that by the end of the day every kid at Kennedy High School will know that there's an art show going on in the library!"

"It's not bad," Jonathan said slowly, a big grin on his face. "As a matter of fact, it's pretty clever, Woody. It would certainly get the show noticed."

"But isn't it just a little bit, um, sensational?" Gloria asked in a sweet voice. "After all, we don't want to detract from the seriousness of the show, do we? We're not putting on a circus, and we ought to promote it in a more dignified way."

"Well, Gloria," Woody said, "we don't really have time to send out engraved invitations."

"You know, Woody," Gloria replied, "people have told you you're funny so often you're starting to believe them."

"Brrr," Woody said, shivering violently and turning up the collar of his plaid flannel shirt. "I just noticed a chill in the air."

Gloria stuck out her tongue.

"Hey, you two, let's not waste our time squabbling. Woody's plan is terrific, and I think we should go with it," Jonathan said. He paused and glanced around the table. Gloria looked away. "So everyone agrees?" The other committee members nodded, with the exception of Gloria. "Okay, now where are we going to find volunteers to be sandwiches?"

"Where else do you look for sandwiches?" Woody said, wiggling his eyebrows. "Right here in the cafeteria. Are we done with our meeting, Jonathan?"

He nodded.

"Then if Pamela will come with me and bring along her notebook," Woody continued, "I bet I can get all the volunteers we need before next period."

Woody led her across the cafeteria to the table in the far corner. Most of the seats were still occupied, though the rest of the room was beginning to empty. She recognized Phoebe and Chris and Ted Mason and his girl friend Molly Ramirez.

125

"Hey, guys," Woody said when they were still a couple of yards away, "I need some volunteers."

"Uh-oh," Ted said. "We'd better go now. We don't want to be late for class." He started to get up, but Woody pushed him back into his chair.

"Sit down, Ted. You have plenty of time. I have something important to say."

He pulled Pamela forward with a flourish. "You all know the art show is coming up next week. Pamela is going to make some magnificent posters for it, something like this" — he produced the open notebook — "and I want volunteers to carry them."

"Carry them?" Phoebe said. "You mean take them around and put them up? I'll be glad to help."

Woody grinned fiendishly and shook his head. "Not put them up, Pheebarooni, *carry* them. March through the halls wearing them around your neck. Still want to help?"

"Well — " She looked around the table and came to a decision. "Sure, why not? It might be a lot of fun."

"May I see?" A tall, lanky boy put out his hand for the notebook. Pamela recognized him as Henry Braverman, the fashion designer. He took the notebook, looked at the cartoon, then gave Pamela a warm smile. "Wow, these are great," he said.

"Thanks."

"What are your poster-carriers going to wear?" he asked.

Woody looked confused. "Clothes, I guess. I

hadn't thought of anything more daring, though it's certainly an interesting idea."

"I quit," Phoebe said. "I said I'd help, but not if it gets me arrested for indecent exposure. Especially not in weather this cold."

"What I meant," Henry said patiently, "was that they ought to be in costume. They're trying to attract attention, after all. Maybe something like old-fashioned artist's smocks and floppy berets."

"Hey, wild!" Woody exclaimed. "And thin, pointy mustaches, right?"

"I like the smock and beret," Phoebe said, "but I will *not* be remembered after graduation as the girl who wore the mustache to school."

"I'll give it a go," Ted said. "I always wanted to twirl a mustache."

Woody gave him a dubious look. "You're supposed to be an artist, you know, not a villain in a melodrama. Think you can handle it, Ted? And who else can I interest in this fine cause?"

Within minutes, he had half a dozen students signed up to parade around on Tuesday wearing smocks, berets, and posters. Henry and his girl friend Janie took responsibility for making the smocks and berets, and Kim Barrie promised to come over on Saturday afternoon to help Pamela make the posters.

By now it really *was* time to go to class. As Pamela was leaving the cafeteria, a girl with long, silky, dark hair and pale, translucent skin caught up with her. "Pamela?" she said in a soft voice. "I'm Sasha Jenkins. Dee Patterson has been telling me all about you."

"Really?" Pamela knew Sasha was the editor of *The Red and the Gold*, the school newspaper.

"Yes. We're planning a special issue of the paper in honor of spring, and I've been thinking that I'd like to illustrate it with line drawings instead of photos. It would make it a lot more special. When Dee showed me the poster you did for the art show, I realized that you'd be just the right person to do the drawings. Would you be interested?"

"Ah, sure," Pamela stammered. "I can't, I mean, right now, I'm just trying to get through the art show. But afterward, sure, I'd love to do it."

"Great. We can talk about it after next week. Your show is generating a lot of interest, by the way. I think it's going to be a big success."

"Oh, I hope so," Pamela said, her eyes sparkling. She really was pleased with all the excitement the show seemed to be generating, and she was glad to have something to take her mind off Matt and Gloria.

# Chapter
## 14

On Wednesday evening Monica was drying her hair when her sister Julie appeared at the door of her bedroom, pointed to her, and pantomimed talking on the telephone. Monica switched off the dryer and said, "Who is it?"

Julie leaned against the side of the doorway and absently scratched her upper arm. "Some guy," she said with a shrug. "It's not Sexy Peter."

"How many times have I told you not to call him that, runt?" Monica stood up and tightened the sash of her terrycloth robe.

Julie stuck out her tongue. "About forty zillion, I guess. Your new guy is still waiting."

The phone was in the hall. Monica aimed a swat at Julie in passing and picked up the receiver. "Hello?" she said.

"Hi, Monica. It's Brent."

"Oh, hi, Brent," she said warmly. "I was just thinking about you."

"How about that, I was just thinking about *you*."

"I really enjoyed watching your recording session. How is the demo coming along?"

"We're just about done mixing it. A few more days should do it. But I'm calling because the Night Owl lost the band they booked for Friday night, and they asked us to do the gig. Want to come give a listen again?"

"This Friday?" She hesitated. "I'd love to, but let me see if Peter has any plans, and I'll get back to you."

"No need, babe. I just got off the phone with him. He's all tied up, but he said you'd probably want to come anyway. Was he right?"

Monica frowned. She and Peter usually spent Friday nights together. Why hadn't he told her that he was going to be busy this Friday?

"Well, I — "

"Tell you what," Brent said. "We're going over to the club around five to set up and do a sound check. Then we'll take a break for a couple of hours before the first show. What if I come by for you around seven-thirty? That'll leave plenty of time before I have to be back at the club."

Somewhere in the back of her mind a voice was saying, "Don't do it." But why on earth not? She wasn't a baby, after all. Now that she had watched the Dial-Tones in the studio, she wanted to see them perform again. The alternative was sitting home alone on Friday night, and she didn't want to do that.

She took a deep breath and said, "Thanks, Brent, that sounds great."

"Good. I'll see you then."

Julie was sitting on the edge of her bed bouncing up and down. She had obviously been listening. "Who's this Brent?" she said slyly. "Does Sexy Peter know about him?"

"He's the lead singer in a rock band, and Peter's the one who introduced me to him, so pooh to you. And don't call him that."

Julie bounced up and stretched, then tucked her T-shirt into her jeans. "Okay," she said innocently. "How about if I call him Hunky Peter instead?" She made it out the door just ahead of the pillow Monica threw at her.

What should she wear for a date with a rock star? Of course it wasn't really a date, she reminded herself as she looked in the mirror for the twentieth time, and Brent wasn't really a star.

She had taken half an hour to decide on a white denim miniskirt and a big shirt with bright geometric designs. Her hair was another problem. She combed it this way and that and finally put it in a topknot tied with a scarf.

Brent showed up exactly at seven-thirty wearing tight black jeans, a shocking-pink T-shirt, a black leather vest, and black cowboy boots. Monica was surprised to find her heart beating rapidly at the sight of him.

"All ready?" Brent asked, holding out his hand.

"Yeah." Monica grabbed her jacket and followed him to the car.

131

He seemed preoccupied during the drive. After getting minimal responses to a couple of comments and questions, Monica settled back in her seat and stared out the window. She suddenly felt uncomfortable sitting here beside Brent, and her thoughts began to turn to Peter.

Things had not been going terribly smoothly between them lately. Earlier in the day she had waited to see him after his lunchtime show, but he had acted as if she were pestering him. And why wasn't he coming with her to hear the Dial-Tones tonight? She had asked him twice. The first time he ignored the question, and the second time he muttered something vague about some new group he needed to hear. If that was really his reason, why hadn't he asked her to come along? He knew that she liked discovering new groups as much as he did.

An awful suspicion crept into her mind and refused to leave. Was Peter seeing someone else? If he was, that might explain his behavior. He had been strangely eager for her to go with Brent tonight. Maybe it set his mind at ease to know she was doing the same thing he was. For a moment she felt a terrible longing to be with Peter. Then she recalled the way Brent had kissed her after the recording session last week and how eagerly she had responded to him. Maybe she and Peter were beginning to drift apart. She was still trying to understand how she felt about that possibility when they pulled up in front of the club.

The place was still empty. Brent looked around at the old, rickety tables and told her to come back to the band's dressing room. She wasn't sure what she expected, but certainly not the bleak, dingy room she found. It was smaller than her room at home, and had concrete floors and cement-block walls. It was furnished with a few broken-down wooden chairs, a small table, some metal hooks to hang clothes on, and one built-in shelf along one wall.

A few minutes later, the other guys in the band showed up with their new roadie, a guy named Billy, and started kidding around with Monica. She liked their jokes and their casual manner. Above all, she liked the easy way they accepted her presence there. When Brent called them together to talk out the order of the first set, she sat in the corner and listened. This was *really* getting to know the music scene from the inside.

Finally, just before it was time to go on, Brent glanced over at her. "Billy," he called, "take Monica out and get her set up at one of the house tables, will you? I'll come out and see you between sets, babe," he said to her. "Enjoy the music."

"You bet." She grinned. "Break a leg!"

He was as good as his word. After a set that had the listeners bouncing in their seats with excitement, Brent appeared from backstage with a towel draped around his neck and sat down across from her. A little crowd gathered around the table, eager to talk to him, including a number of fellow musicians who had come to check out the band. He introduced her to those he knew as "Monica, a *primo* DJ," which made her feel grateful and accepted. It instantly promoted her from part of the decor to a member of the club.

Billy came out to join her for the first part of the second set. Between songs, she discovered that he had total faith in the Dial-Tones' future. "Brent has an in with a rich dude who flipped over the demo," he explained. "He's dickering for enough development bucks to put together a whole album at once. And this very big video freak from New York caught the act a couple of weeks ago and is doing a conceptual script for 'Climb My Oak.' They could start shooting by the end of April." He smiled. "Guess I'll stick with them as a roadie for a while."

"I'll say. Hey, that's fantastic news about the video," Monica said. "Can I pass any of that along?"

"Hey, no," Billy said, looking around. "Everything's at a very sensitive place right now. One wrong look and it could all go boom! I really shouldn't have said anything about it at all."

"Don't worry, I can keep quiet." She smiled reassuringly and turned her attention back to the band.

The second set got an even stronger reception than the first. The audience simply wouldn't let the band leave the stage, even after three encores. Finally Brent came out, mopping his face, and told them that he had to go — the helicopter was waiting outside. Most of the audience laughed good-naturedly. The rest apparently took him seriously and looked very impressed.

She waited a few minutes, then went backstage.

Ten or fifteen people were milling in the hall outside the dressing room, waiting to see the guys in the band. When Brent came out, a few of them cheered. The black leather had been packed away; he was in blue jeans and a faded Grateful Dead T-shirt now. He looked around for her and pulled her over for a hug.

She gave him a peck on the cheek. "Fantastic show," she said. "You were all right there the whole time."

He nodded. "It happens sometimes. I wish I knew how to *make* it happen." Then he turned away, his arm still around her, and started talking to one of the fans.

Almost half an hour passed before he was finally ready to leave. By that time Monica was feeling tired and hungry. After listening to ten people all say pretty much the same things to Brent, she was also just a tiny bit bored. But hadn't somebody described the day of a rock musician on tour as two hours of incredible exhilaration and twenty-two hours of waiting for those two hours?

"I'm starved," he said, once they were in the car. "What about you?"

"Mm-hmm. It's been a long time since dinner. Do you know what there is around here?"

"Around here? *Nada.* You just left the only bright spot in the whole burg. But I filled my fridge just this morning. Let's go by my place, and we can whip something up together."

She sat up a little straighter in her seat. "No, thanks," she said carefully, "I don't think so. I know a couple of places in Rose Hill that will still be open. What about if we go to one of them?"

His manner still seemed casual, but she sensed some tension gathering beneath it. "Why waste money in some grease joint when we can do so much better by ourselves? Come with me and see if I'm not right."

"No, thanks," she said again. "As a matter of fact, I'm really too tired to eat anything now, anyway. I'd like to go home."

"That's a shame," he said lightly. "You see, my car is a creature of habit. After a gig, it drives to my place. If you really want to go somewhere else, I guess you'll have to find some other way to get there."

Monica swallowed. She had never thought that she'd find herself in a situation like this one. She heard of it happening to other girls and always wondered how the girl had been stupid enough to get into it in the first place. Now she understood. It didn't require stupidity, just a blind spot. Quite a few things about Brent should have sent her a warning signal, but Monica had ignored these things because he was a rock musician. He was *supposed* to act that way. It hadn't occurred to her that it might not be an act.

She swallowed again, cleared her throat, and said, "That's pretty funny, Brent, but seriously, I want to go home now."

"Come on, Monica. What are you afraid of?"

She wanted to grab Brent's arm and plead with him to drive her home. She also wanted to sock him in the face, really hard. Her common sense, still functioning in spite of her rising panic, told her that either impulse would be a total disaster. But what was she going to do?

She looked around the empty parking lot and started to shiver. The neighborhood was strange, dark, and foreboding. There wasn't a living soul in sight. It was almost as if they had wandered onto an abandoned movie set of a tough urban area. She could get out of the car and go in search of a payphone, but she didn't want to take that chance around here.

She would rather take her chance with Brent.

Her breath was coming fast and shallow, and she was sure that he could sense her fear. Then she remembered her conversation with Billy. Could she use it somehow?

"You know, Brent," she said, as calmly as she could, "I really do think you ought to take me home now."

"No. My place or nowhere." He sat back and crossed his arms, with a hint of a grin on his face.

She chose her words very carefully. She didn't dare insult him so much that he got angry, but she had to make sure that he got her point very clearly. "Would that be sensible, Brent? You've got a chance to make it very big. You know that, and so do I. But the music business is funny. Even the littlest thing can throw a career off track for good. It's all run by businessmen, you know. They hate bad publicity because it costs them money. One strong hint of bad news and they catch the next plane back to New York, and there you are, hung out to dry. You don't want that to happen to you, and neither do I."

She had watched him out of the corner of her eye while she was speaking. He had lost the grin after the first few words, and when she mentioned New York, he had stared at her with an intensity that almost paralyzed her tongue. For a long moment after she finished, he seemed to be caught up in a debate with himself. She waited, taut as a guitar string, to find out which side won.

"Hhmph," he finally said. "I guess I'd better take you home after all."

She didn't reply. She wasn't after an apology, or understanding, or a reconciliation. All she wanted was to get home as quickly and safely as she could, and then to forget that Brent existed.

He wasn't very talkative, either. When he pulled up in front of her house, he maintained a sullen silence.

She couldn't leave it like that. "Well," she said, "the music was terrific. And I do think you have a great future." She got out of the car, then held the door open long enough to add, "I also think you acted like a first-class pig tonight. And I really wish you hadn't!"

She slammed the door as hard as she could and ran up the walk. When she reached her front door, she burst out in sobs. The outburst did not relieve her feelings at all, only made her more aware of their intensity. She hated Brent for scaring her like that and for not acting like the guy she had thought he was. He had completely ruined what, up until then, had been a fantastic evening. And she was maddest of all at Peter Lacey. What had happened was more his fault than anyone's. He had set her up like a target in a shooting gallery. All Brent had done was accept the invitation to take a shot. She didn't care if she was being rational or not. Peter had pushed her into this and she never wanted to see him again.

# *Chapter*
# *15*

Pamela had three drawings spread out on the table. The first was of a brick fireplace with an antique rocker in front of it. The second showed a single bare tree in the midst of a snow-covered field. And the third, her favorite, was of an old broken-down tractor sitting in waist-high grass at the edge of a meadow. Though three different students had drawn them, she was positive that they belonged together. But how to place them so they supported each other, rather than drew attention away from each other?

She was shifting them into still another arrangement when Fiona came over. "Pamela, do you know where your father might be? I've just put up those four portraits, and something is distinctly not right about them. Woody walked by, looked at them, and began to laugh."

"That's not unusual for him," Pamela said with a smile.

"Perhaps not, but when I asked for his reason, he refused to explain. I would much rather not provide the show with unintended comedy if I can help it."

Pamela looked around the library. The line of bulletin boards down the center on which they were mounting the artwork made it difficult to locate her dad. Then she saw him near the door, chatting with Kim Barrie. She pointed him out and went back to moving her three drawings around.

A few minutes later her father was by the door again. He noticed her glance and motioned her over. "You have a nice bunch of friends," he began. "I've really enjoyed meeting them."

"Thanks, Dad. I'm glad you could come down. Did you figure out what was wrong with Fiona's display?"

"The English girl?" He started to chuckle. "She had hung the portraits so that it looked as if they were staring suspiciously at each other. We got it straightened out, though."

He put his hands in his pockets and looked casually around the room. "And the girl I was just talking to?" he continued. "Kim? Do you know about Earthly Delights, her mother's catering business?"

"Sure, I've heard of it. Why?"

"According to Kim, they've been thinking about doing very luxurious boxed gourmet picnics for Wolf Trap this summer, but they haven't been able to work out the right sort of packaging for them. I gave Kim my card and a few ideas that popped into my mind. I have a hunch her mother may give me a call one of these days."

"Mixing business and pleasure, Dad? Tut, tut."

"Nonsense. Do you know any other way to keep business fun?"

"I guess not," she laughed. "And I'd better go mind *my* business, instead of standing around talking."

"In a minute." He took her arm and led her toward the table near the door. "I wanted to ask you if you'd seen this."

It was a model of a futuristic automobile, sculpted in clay. The lines of the automobile had been distorted in such a way that it seemed to speed across the field of vision. Pamela almost felt that if she blinked for too long, it would have vanished around a corner by the time she opened her eyes. "No, I didn't," she replied. "It must have been submitted to one of the other committee members."

"So you don't know who did it?"

She shook her head. "I can ask around and find out, if you like. What's the matter? It is sort of technical, I guess. Do you think it doesn't belong in the show?"

As she spoke, she noticed some movement behind her dad. She looked over his shoulder and saw Matt standing in the doorway listening to them. His khaki work clothes had oil smudges on them, and his knuckles were grimy. From the way his jaw was set, she could tell he was in a rage. She had the urge to run to him and put her arms around him and make everything all right. But as usual, his hard gaze made her keep her distance.

Before her father could answer her question, Matt stepped between them and picked up the model. "Don't worry," he said roughly. "I'm not going to spoil your precious art show with this. I should have known Jonathan was up to something when he asked if he could borrow it."

"Uh, Dad," Pamela said hastily, "This is Matt Jacobs. Matt, this is my father."

"Glad to meet you, Matt. You ought to be careful with that. It's pretty fragile, you know."

"I know it is," Matt said grimly. "But I'm not going to leave it where it isn't welcome. I'm taking it home right now."

"Are you the artist?"

Matt blinked with surprise at the word, and said, "I made it, yes."

"Did you design it, too?"

"You mean is it a real car? No, just something I dreamed up. I've always liked drawing cars, and a while back I started doing them in modeling clay, too."

"It shows a lot of skill and imagination," Pamela's father said.

Pamela was starting to feel left out of the conversation. "Daddy's a graphic designer," she said brightly.

Matt gave her a sullen glance and looked away. Had she said something wrong?

"Have you ever thought about going for a career in industrial design, Matt?" her father said.

The question seemed to throw him. "Me? Uh, no, sir, I haven't. I don't know anything about the field. I like working on cars. This is just something I fiddle around with in my spare time."

Pamela glanced around. Jonathan was hovering a few feet away, looking worried.

"Well, you ought to give it some thought," her father continued. "It's a very big field these days, and always in need of new talent. It looks to me as though you might have what it takes to succeed in it."

Matt's confusion deepened. He looked around as if expecting somebody to rescue him. "I — I'd better go now," he said. "I've got a lot of homework to do tonight." He took a step backward and seemed about to bolt out the door.

Pamela came to a sudden decision. "Oh no, you don't!" She reached over and plucked the model out of his hands. For a second he seemed about to resist, but then he relaxed his grip.

"You can leave if you want, Matt," she said, "but this stays here. It belongs in the art show. And shame on you for not knowing it yourself and making your friend submit it for you."

"Hey, I didn't. . . . It was *his* idea! I didn't even know about it." He tentatively held out his hands, but Pamela kept the model perched in her palms and looked at him defiantly.

"Oh, never mind," he said. As he turned to go, he caught sight of Jonathan. "I'll deal with you later," he added, glowering at his friend. Then he walked out without another word. Pamela couldn't help thinking he looked pleased, though. She noticed the hint of a smile had played at his lips when she took the model from him.

"Well," her father said. "Let's see if we can't find a conspicuous place for that piece. I think it's one of the best in the show, and I've seen a lot of fine work here tonight."

As Pamela followed her father about the library looking for a spot for the model car, the animation she had felt while talking to Matt was beginning to fade, leaving a familiar sense of despair in its place. Once she had thought that they would be friends, or maybe even more than friends. But lately nothing had gone right between them. Why did he seem so mad at her all the time?

# Chapter
# 16

"Okay, Cardinals, in anticipation of a holiday that's coming our way soon, here's a moldy oldie that belongs in everybody's collection. It's Frankie Lymon and the Teenagers asking the age-old question, 'Why Do Fools Fall in Love?'"

Monica stabbed her spoon into her yogurt container, causing a tiny geyser of blueberry juice to erupt from the bottom. She muttered under her breath and reached for a napkin. The week had been totally awful so far, but lunchtime was the absolute worst. It was still too cold to eat out in the quad, and any place else she went she heard Peter's cheerful, wisecracking voice. How could he possibly sound so happy when she was so miserable?

They hadn't said a word to each other since her disastrous evening with Brent. The first time she saw him, she had still been too angry to speak, and the second time, when she was almost ready to talk to him, he had walked right by and pretended not to see her. She had had to fight the impulse to run after him and bean him with her history textbook, which weighed about seventeen pounds. It wasn't fair at all. She had every right to be mad at him, but why was he mad at *her*?

By now they had settled into a routine. Whenever they found themselves in the same room, they exchanged a few uneasy glances, then waited sullenly for the other to make the first move. Monica didn't think it should be up to her to break the silence. Peter was acting as if she'd done something wrong.

"There we have it, boys and girls," Peter's smooth, confident voice said over the four-part harmony that concluded the song. "And the best answer to Little Frankie's question, in twenty-five words or less, will get a prize. Five, yes, five song requests on my show, with my personal guarantee to play them if I can find them. So if you have a secret desire to listen to Steely Dan or to hear the Trashmen doing 'The Surfing Bird,' get the bubblegum out of your ears and listen up. This is your chance to overrule my good taste and discrimination. Send your entries to me, Peter Lacey, care of WKND, and get them in soon, before I recover my sanity and call the whole thing off."

Monica had to smile. Peter had a gift for dreaming up these spur-of-the-moment gimmicks. Sometimes they worked and sometimes they fell over with a thud. This sounded like one he could milk for days, reading entries on the air, getting kids to vote for their favorite, then doing a job on the song choices of the unfortunate winner. With a little luck he would have the whole school talking about the contest and looking forward eagerly to his show.

"Okay," he continued, "now for something really special. I opened my mailbox yesterday and there was a cassette of a demo just cut a couple of weeks ago by a new group right here from our area."

Monica's hands became fists and her nails began to dig into her palms.

"Take it from me, Cardinals, these guys are going to be big. Years from now, when you're sitting around tuned to an easy-listening station, you'll still talk about the day you first heard this group, right here on KND. So here they are, the Dial-Tones doing 'Climb My Oak.'"

As the familiar intro filled the cafeteria, Monica shoved her chair back and jumped to her feet. This was too much. If Peter thought he could get away with insulting and humiliating her like this, she was going to teach him a lesson right now!

The outer door to the studio was unlocked. Monica charged through into the room, then skidded to a halt when she saw the red light was on over the control room door. As mad as she was, she couldn't bring herself to barge into the control room while he was on the air. A live, unrehearsed fight over the air would certainly get attention, but afterward she would have to change her name and move to Wyoming.

But *was* he on the air? He could easily be sitting there twiddling his thumbs in front of a dead mike while the song was playing. He was probably congratulating himself for being the first to broadcast Brent's song. There had to be a monitor somewhere in this room — in fact, she knew there was, but where was it? She scanned the walls near the ceiling without success. Then she saw it, an old wooden speaker box sitting on the battered desk in the corner. She reached over and turned up the volume control on the side.

Peter's voice emerged. ". . . who like to discover new trends, new groups, new sounds. We at KND are always out looking for what you want to hear, whether it's new, old, or in between. And here's a cut I've gotten a lot of requests for. It's by a guy from New Jersey I think you all know."

The instant that Springsteen started playing, Monica opened the control room door. Peter was standing by the board, looking through a stack of albums and dancing away. He looked around in surprise. "Hey, you . . ." he began. When he saw it was Monica, his face fell. "Oh, it's you," he said glumly. "Close the door, would you?"

She had been looking forward to shouting and carrying on, but suddenly there didn't seem to be any point. "I came here to tell you two things, Peter," she said calmly. "I'm through with the station and I'm through with you."

His face reddened and his mouth fell open. "Just like that? If you don't want to discuss it, why didn't you just send me a postcard? Is that all you have to say?"

"Don't you worry, I have plenty more to say. I just don't feel like wasting my breath on you, that's all."

"Really? Or maybe you're afraid that if you say it out loud, you'll have to see — oops!" His skilled fingers quickly faded the turntable and brought up the level on the mike. "A song from the Boss to carry you through the afternoon," he said smoothly as he cued up another record on turntable B. "And now here's a cut from a band that is making a very big name for itself in its home country of Ireland, a band that calls itself Moving Hearts."

He brought up the music and killed the mike, then wheeled around. "What's the matter with you? Bursting in here in the middle of a show like this."

"That's the most important thing in the world to you, isn't it? Peter Lacey, star DJ, and his almighty show on WKND! I always knew you'd do anything for your show, but I guess I never realized how far *anything* stretches."

"And I always suspected you'd do anything to get ahead. I didn't know how right I was! Excuse me." He brushed past her through the door to the record library and returned a moment later with a couple more albums in his hand. He was just in time to catch the end of the Irish group's song.

"There you have it, all you Irish rock fans, a band called Moving Hearts. And I'm not going to try out my brogue on you, because if I did, I'd have an indignant crowd throwing potatoes at me when I leave the station after the show. Right now, a classic from one of the early albums by the world's greatest rock and roll band, The Rolling Stones."

He gave her an evil grin as the first bars of "Stupid Girl" resounded through the studio and all over Kennedy High School.

"Very funny," she said acidly.

He spread his hands in a gesture of innocence. "Hey, I didn't give it a dedication, did I? I just can't believe the way you played right into that guy's hands, Monica. You expect me to be happy about it? It was low."

She had thought that she was already as angry as she could get, but now she found out what was meant by a towering rage. "Low!" she shouted. "You try to pass me along to some creep because you think he can help your career, and you have the nerve to call *me* low? All *I* did was refuse to go along with your plans!"

"Is that so! Then what do you call breaking up with the guy you've been going with for months, just because some dude walks by who might be a star some day? I know I'm not a musician and never will be. I know in your book I'm probably down as an untalented hanger-on. But I still deserved fairer treatment than I got."

"Fairer treatment! Was it fair when you — "

The Stones song had reached its final bars. Peter held up his hand, and Monica shut up at once.

"Awright!" he said into the microphone. "And before I get buried under a pile of protest letters, I'd better point out that the song is only about one particular girl, and not about girls in general. Okay? Now let's stay on the British side of the pond for this next song from Dire Straits. Hit it, guys!"

The interruption gave Monica a few moments to think. Since when was Peter so hung up about not being a musician? Who cared? He was a funny, sensitive, loving, and yes, *very* good-looking guy, not to mention a talented DJ. So what if he couldn't play "Chopsticks" without making half a dozen mistakes? He also couldn't tapdance, solve complicated equations in his head, or throw a winning pass from the thirty-yard line. None of that mattered to her. She loved him for just being him.

A horrid suspicion grew on her. She had to check it out. The moment the mike was off, she said, "Peter, why do you think I'm breaking up with you?"

He refused to meet her eye. Picking up a stack of albums, he started toward the music library without answering.

She followed him to the door. "I mean it, Peter. I want to know."

He shrugged with his back still on her. "The usual reason. You got a better offer." He began to put the albums back in their proper slots. She noticed that his hand was trembling.

"You think I'm going with *Brent*?"

"Aren't you? You were with him on Friday night, and ever since, you've been trying to pretend I don't exist. Of course you're going with him. What girl wouldn't? He's going to be a star."

Her sense of frustration made her slam her fist against the door. It hurt. She stepped closer to Peter, rubbing the edge of her hand. "Peter Lacey," she said, "you are a total idiot. I wouldn't fall for Brent if he were Bruce Springsteen and Mick Jagger and Jim Morrison all rolled into one! The reason I'm so mad is that you tried to set me up with that jerk!"

"Set you up?" He looked over his shoulder at her.

"Well, what would *you* call it?" she went on, refusing to yield the floor until she had said what she had to say. "Leaving me at the recording session for him to bring me home! Telling him that you were busy on Friday, but *I'd* love to come hear his group! And ever since we met him you've been going on about Brent this and Brent that and what a terrific guy he is, until I was sick of hearing it!"

"I was jealous," Peter said in such a low voice she had to strain to hear him.

"*Jealous*? Of Brent? You sure picked a funny way to show it!"

He finally turned to face her. "Come on, Monica, I didn't want to stand in your way. Once I saw how he talked to you and how you watched him up on stage, I knew I didn't have a chance. I wouldn't exactly say I set you up with him. But why make everyone miserable for nothing? So I —"

He stopped talking suddenly. His jaw dropped and he turned so pale that she thought he might be about to faint.

"Monica," he said in a voice that turned her blood to ice. "Did you touch that door?"

"Huh?" She whirled around. The door just behind her was firmly shut. "I don't think so." She grabbed the knob and twisted it, but she knew the awful truth already. They were trapped.

"My show!" he exclaimed. "I'm still on the air!"

"Good," she said. "In a couple of minutes

somebody will come to see what force of nature was able to shut you up."

"Very funny. I swear, this afternoon I'm coming back here with a screwdriver to take that door off its hinges."

Monica started to laugh. This was the third time she and Peter had gotten themselves trapped by that door. Was anybody going to believe that it had been accidental every time?

"Maybe you'd better leave it up," she said, putting her hands on his shoulders. "We may need it the next time we misunderstand each other so badly. And don't think just because I love you that I'm forgiving you so easily. You still have a whole lot of explaining to do."

"Yeah? Well, don't think just because *I* love *you*, I'm forgiving *you* so easily, either. You fell pretty hard into the trap you say I set."

"I *say* — " Monica began.

"But we've got lots of time." Peter leaned over to kiss her lightly, then again, not so lightly. "Lots of time," he repeated. "I just remembered. That Dire Straits number I put on was the first cut on that side. No one will start worrying about me for at least fifteen minutes."

# *Chapter 17*

Pamela stood by the window and looked anxiously down the street. Brenda was five minutes late. She hoped Brenda hadn't forgotten that she was supposed to pick her up. This was too important an evening to miss. Important and scary. Tony had taken her aside on Saturday morning to tell her about tonight.

"I like our volunteers to know what the kids they're working with are going through," he explained. "The group experience is one of the most important elements in our program here. It gives the kids the feeling of support and connection they need to cope with problems that are still too much for them to deal with alone."

Remembering his words, she felt tears welling up in her eyes. The kids at Garfield House weren't the only ones trying to cope with problems, and feeling alone and helpless. She had ventured out of the safe confines of her studio in the hope of becoming closer to people her own age, and she had to admit that it had worked in part. But was it worth it? Look what had happened with Matt. Hadn't she been happier before she met him?

She gripped the edge of the curtain tightly. What happened at these group sessions? Were they going to force her to share her intimate feelings with people she didn't know? Or worse yet, with people she *did* know and saw every week, even every day? The prospect terrified her, yet had a kind of fascinating appeal, too.

A loud honk brought her out of her reverie. She grabbed her coat and hurried out to the car.

"Did you get Tony's note?" Brenda asked as they pulled away from the curb.

"About the training group?" Pamela said. "No, he told me about it, though. I thought of skipping it. It's kind of scary, don't you think?"

"It is the first couple of times, but it's also a very important thing for us to experience."

"That's what Tony said, too."

Brenda took her hand off the wheel long enough to pat her arm. "It's normal to be scared, Pamela," Brenda said, sensing her friend's nervousness. "I was petrified my first time. And these groups *can* get very intense sometimes, but you really don't have to be afraid. Everyone is there to help everyone else. Nobody gets torn down or ganged up on. If the mood starts to get too negative, Tony'll step in and turn it around."

"Oh." She relaxed just a little bit. She didn't really know Tony well, but she sensed that he was someone she could trust. Then a thought came that made her more nervous than ever. "Will all the volunteers be there?"

Brenda laughed. "We don't have a room big enough for that. Anyway, a training group has to be pretty small to work properly. No, this one is just for those of us who are usually there on Wednesday nights. You, me, Matt, Gloria, David, and Colleen. And Tony, of course."

Pamela swallowed. "I think I feel sick," she said in a small voice. "I want to go home."

After a shrewd glance, Brenda said, "It's too late for that. We're practically there. Don't worry, Pamela, you'll be fine. Just don't be afraid to let your real self show. Trying to fake it is the one really dangerous thing you can do in a group."

Good advice, maybe, but how could she possibly follow it? There was so much she couldn't say, so many topics she had to skirt. If she talked at all about her feelings for Matt, she wouldn't be able to hide her jealousy of Gloria. And that would be the same as revealing the secret that she had promised to keep, that Matt and Gloria were seeing each other. It wasn't so much breaking her promise to Gloria that bothered her — looking back, she realized that Gloria had practically trapped her into it. But she couldn't risk the consequences for Matt.

Tony was standing in the hall when they came in. "Hi, gang," he said cheerfully. "We're going to meet in the room right next to my office. Oh, Brenda, could I see you for a minute first?"

Pamela walked into the room feeling like the main attraction at a sacrificial rite. Seven chairs were set up in a tight circle. Matt and Gloria were already there, sitting next to each other. Pamela gave them a weak smile and a nod and sat down on the opposite side of the circle, next to David, whom she didn't know at all. Tony came in a moment later, followed by Brenda and Colleen, a pretty black girl who taught a dance class. Brenda sat down in the empty seat beside Pamela.

"Okay," Tony said, "a couple of ground rules for the group. The first is that nothing that's said in this room goes out of this room. That's absolutely crucial. Do all of you agree to that?" He paused and looked around the circle. When his eyes met Pamela's, she nodded seriously. He completed the circuit and said, "Good. Second rule: You can say anything you feel like about yourself or about any of the rest of us, but you have to realize that everyone else has the same right. If anybody gets into a shouting match, I reserve the right to step in and move us to a more constructive place. Is that clear?"

Pamela nodded again and surreptitiously dried her palms on her jeans. What now? Was Tony going to call on them to talk? As a precaution, she kept her gaze fixed firmly on the rug in the middle of the circle. She felt as if she were back in fourth grade and had come to school without doing her homework.

"Right," he said. "One of the things I hope we'll get into is how you feel about your work here at Garfield House; what's right and what's wrong and what we can all do to help each other. But to start off, how are you feeling about being here, in this room, right now? David?"

Pamela gulped. He *was* calling on people.

"I'm so scared I can hardly catch my breath," David said. "I don't like to talk to *anyone* about what I'm feeling and I hate being put in this situation. How do I know I can trust you people? You all seem nice, but I don't know you."

"I know exactly what you mean," Brenda said. "I felt the same way the first time I was in one of these groups, and I always feel that way when we're just getting started. It's hard to open up, because it makes you vulnerable. But if we're all really committed to helping and supporting each other, then we all have the same stake in making it work."

"Brenda," Tony said, "aren't you being a little too theoretical? Talk from your experience."

Pamela stole a glance at Brenda. Her face was pale and tight, and Pamela suddenly realized that this was hard for her, too. The knowledge comforted her.

"All right," Brenda said after a silence. "There's something I haven't been looking at that I need help with. And it has to do with some of you. When Tony asked me to take charge of the volunteer program, I was really proud and happy. I wanted to do the best job I could, not only for Garfield House but even more as a way of showing Tony how much I respect him. And maybe I thought it was a way to earn Tony's respect, or that by becoming really important to the program, I'd make sure that he wouldn't stop needing me."

Her voice was steady, but when Pamela looked at her again, she saw tears glistening in her eyes.

"I know why that's off base," Brenda continued, "and I'm working on it. But what I want to say here is that I've been trying so hard to make the volunteer program a success that I've stopped paying attention to the people who make it up. Instead of making the program fit better with their needs and feelings, I've pushed and shoved to make them fit into what *I* thought the program needed."

She turned and looked straight at Pamela. "I keep saying 'them,' " she said, "but what I really mean is 'you.' I've imposed on you, manipulated you, and tried to ignore what I knew you were feeling, all to make *my* program a success. I shouldn't have done that, and I'm really sorry I did."

As she finished, her voice broke. Wordlessly Pamela reached out and put her arms around her.

After a long moment, Brenda straightened up and smiled at her through her tears. "I can't say I won't make the same mistake again," she said, "but from now on I'll be watching for it."

"David," Tony said, "what were you thinking just now, while Brenda was speaking?"

David blushed. "Well . . . I was moved by what she said and really impressed that she could talk about it so openly." His voice trailed off.

Listening to David, Pamela suddenly found herself wanting to talk about her concerns. Quickly, before her courage could ebb again, she said, "I've been planning to drop out of the program and leave Garfield House."

Everyone turned to look at her. Bashfulness overwhelmed her.

When she didn't continue, Tony prompted her. "Why, Pamela? Is this connected to what Brenda was saying?"

"Oh no, it's nothing like that. Brenda pushed me a little, but mostly she's supportive. No, it's a personal thing. I — " She broke off and tried to think how to say it without betraying Matt and Gloria. Maybe there wasn't any way.

"There's somebody that I thought I was getting really close to," she said, carefully avoiding everyone's eyes. "Or maybe just wanted to get close to, because sometimes he got very distant and I couldn't tell why. Then he . . . he got involved with somebody else. After that it seemed like he couldn't care less about me. It really hurt. I thought he liked me, but if he did, how could he act so coldly toward me?"

She dabbed at her eyes fast with the back of her hand. "I don't like feeling hurt, and I don't like feeling jealous," she continued. "I *hate* it. But whenever I'm around them, that's how they make me feel. So I just decided, to avoid feeling like that, it would be better to stay away. That's all."

She clasped her hands in her lap and stared down at them. She knew that she had just given herself away, and for what? What could anybody say to her except, "Gee, hard luck"?

"This guy you want to be close to," Colleen said, "have you told him how you feel? Does he know he hurt you?"

Pamela shook her head. She was relieved that Colleen didn't seem to know who she was talking about. "No, how could I tell him? I'd sound like such a fool."

"Has he talked to you about what *he's* feeling?"

"No," she repeated. "We haven't talked at all since — "

"Since you made up your mind that he was only interested in somebody else and dropped him without any explanation," David interrupted. Even while Pamela grappled with his words, she wondered if he was thinking about something similar that had happened to him.

"That's not fair! I didn't drop him, I. . . ." She stopped in confusion. *Had* she dropped Matt? Or might it have seemed to him that she had? She could no longer remember exactly what had happened. She was dying to see how Matt was reacting, but she didn't dare look up.

"Pamela," Brenda said, "the only way to get straight with this thing is to be completely open with the other person. Let him know what's going on with you, then see how he reacts. As it is, you don't know what his reactions mean, because you don't know what *he* thinks is going on."

"That's right," Colleen said. "You've got to represent yourself to him. It may hurt like anything if he backs away or rejects you, but at least you'll know what's going on. The way things are going, you're just wandering around in the dark."

"I don't agree," Gloria said. Pamela tensed at the sound of her voice. Why had she brought this whole thing up? "What's the point of going after something you know you can't have? If this guy isn't interested, so much the worse for him. You

162

don't owe him openness or anything else. Go find someone else, that's all."

"That's okay as far as it goes," David said. "But what we're saying is that Pamela doesn't really know if the guy's interested or not. And unless she tells him how she's feeling, she won't ever know. We're not saying to be open for his sake, we're saying be open for your own sake."

"Well, I think that's stupid. Why show all your cards?" Gloria said. "If you play your hand right, you stand a chance of getting what you're after. Otherwise, forget it."

"Wow!" Colleen exclaimed. "You've really got it down, don't you? Play it cool, don't show your feelings, just hope that things are going to go your way. Don't ever reveal what you want, just hope people will realize from your actions. No way. You just eat yourself up thinking that way."

Gloria's face was pale. "Oh, come on," she said in a strained voice. "You mean you never tried to impress somebody? Told them what they wanted to hear, acted the way they wanted you to act? I think it's the only way. Give people what they want and they'll do what you want."

"That's not what you're doing now, is it?" Tony pointed out. "Why is that?"

She jumped to her feet. "Because I don't *want* anything from you, that's why. You're just a bunch of losers, all of you. But I'm *not* a loser and I'm not going to let myself get sucked into this fake emotional routine."

"Gloria, I'm hearing an awful lot of anger behind your words. If all you mean is that you disagree with us, you could just say that. Why are you fighting so hard? Who are you arguing with?" Tony asked.

"Who? You! You and all the rest of them! You act so smug and virtuous and buddy-buddy, and all the time you're doing your best to keep me down and lock me out! But I know why. You're determined not to let me show you up. You think if you make me feel left out long enough, I'll give up and fade away. Well, you're wrong. Just wait, you'll see. I'll show all of you!"

As she ran to the door and fumbled with the knob, Tony said, "Gloria, are you sure you want to leave like this? We're here to talk about these things. Wouldn't it be better to stay and work it out rather than be angry at all of us?"

"Just leave me alone!" Gloria shouted, on the verge of tears. "None of you has ever been nice to me, and now isn't the time to start." She finally succeeded in opening the door and practically flew out of the room.

Pamela felt deeply shaken, as if a bottomless crevice had suddenly opened up inside her. She looked around and found that the others seemed just as disturbed. Tony was especially upset.

"I'm really sorry she walked out," he said, "and I think I have to take some of the blame. I should have seen how much conflict she was feeling and handled her differently."

"You couldn't," Brenda said. "Gloria worked so hard at presenting an image that you couldn't have known what was really going on. Gloria works hard at putting up a front."

Pamela nodded. She was going to have to go

back and take another look at everything Gloria had ever said to her. Was any of it true, or was it all just part of a complex maneuver? "Tony?" she said hesitantly. "Is there a rule here about volunteers being — I mean, getting close to each other? Dating?"

He looked surprised. "No, of course not. We don't encourage our volunteers to get too involved with the kids who are staying here, because they're usually in too much emotional turmoil to be entirely responsible, but what volunteers do on their own time is their own business. Why?"

"It doesn't matter." She retreated into her thoughts, which seemed to lead around in circles and end up back where they started. The sound of Matt's voice finally snapped her out of her speculations. "My fingernails are always dirty," she thought she heard him say.

She shook her head to clear her thoughts. She must have heard wrong. What on earth could he be talking about?

"They aren't really," he continued, "but I always feel like they are. Like I don't belong with people who keep their hands clean."

"You can't work on engines and keep your hands clean," Tony observed neutrally.

"I know that. What I mean is, I feel like everybody looks down on me because I'm a mechanic. A grease monkey. A while ago I got sort of involved with this girl I know at school. I think she really liked me, too, but she ended up going back to her old boyfriend, the son of a congressman. I keep thinking that if I wasn't just some kid who worked in a gas station, if I hadn't been so far beneath the other guy, she might have acted differently."

Pamela was instantly furious with this unknown girl who had treated Matt badly and hurt him so much. How could anyone be so insensitive? But then she remembered how she had felt when she first saw the boxes of tools and spare parts in the back seat of the Camaro. Hadn't she automatically assumed in some corner of her mind that its owner would be slow-witted and insensitive?

"But Matt," David began.

"Wait a second," Matt said. "What I want to say is that in the past few weeks I've realized something I never knew before. I've been a big part of that feeling of being looked down on. I've bought into it and helped make it happen. I've even caught myself staying away from people who seemed too cultured for me. I don't know how I can stop doing that, but I know I have to try. It's costing me too much."

As he said this, he looked straight at Pamela, and a shiver ran down her spine.

"What's wrong with being a good mechanic?" Colleen demanded. "The kids I've talked to think your class is terrific."

He blushed just enough for Pamela to notice, and she didn't know how much longer she could refrain from going over to him, throwing her arms around his neck, and telling him exactly how she felt about him. He looked so sweet and vulnerable sitting there. She longed to comfort him.

"I don't think there's anything wrong with being a mechanic," Matt responded, "but what I have to learn is that it's up to me to validate it.

I've got to stop being so down on myself and I've got to stop thinking that everyone else judges me for what I'm interested in."

"I think that's a very important thing to know," Tony said. "And not just for you. For all of us."

# Chapter
## 18

By the end of the group meeting, Pamela felt as if she had been sitting around a campfire with her oldest and closest friends.

From across the room, Matt met her eyes, then looked away shyly. She watched him for a few moments longer, her heart beating furiously, then stood up and walked over to him. "Matt?" she said hesitantly. "Can you give me a ride home? I have some things I'd like to talk to you about."

"Uh, sure," he muttered, not quite meeting her eyes. "I guess I'd like to talk to you, too."

They walked the two blocks to the car in silence, both wrapped in their own thoughts. Matt unlocked the passenger door and held it open for Pamela. She got in and leaned over to unlock his door, then sat up straight and gathered her courage.

The moment he closed his door, and before he could start the engine, she said, "Matt, I was talking about you back there." Matt didn't turn the key in the ignition. Obviously he had something to say, too. Pamela stared at her feet.

"I thought you might have been," he said quietly. "I hoped you were. I see a lot of things now I didn't understand before tonight, don't you?"

"You were talking about me, too, weren't you? Have I really been acting like such a terrible snob? I didn't mean to. I can't help loving art, but I don't think I'm better than other people because of it."

"It wasn't your fault," he said quickly. "That's exactly what I was talking about. The minute you told me about your painting, and how your whole family is artistic, I figured that you were bound to look down on me. But that was because *I* was looking down on me. When you pulled your disappearing act, I figured you'd finally realized that I wasn't worth your while. But then, I saw you with your dad, and I knew I'd been wrong. I still don't understand what happened, but I know what *didn't*."

She turned to face him. The streetlamp cast a bar of light across his face and captured the glimmer in his eyes. "I can explain all that," she said.

"Not now," he whispered. He reached out and touched her cheek with his palm, and she leaned the weight of her head against it, feeling his strength holding her up. Then she was in his arms, kissing him, and it felt familiar and so right.

How long had she dreamed of this? How many hours had she spent staring into the dark night, wondering if it would ever happen? She thought she might burst with happiness. She lost herself in his kiss and felt his arms tighten around her. As she let her hand glide over the long smooth muscles of his back, she suddenly realized that he had been wanting this as badly as she had. How had they ever miscommunicated to such an extent that she had been so miserable? Well, it didn't matter now. Nothing mattered except that she was in his arms at last.

"Pamela?" he said finally.

"Yes?"

"I'm so glad that this happened tonight. You don't know how long I've been wanting to tell you how I feel about you."

"Shh, Matt. I know, I know," she said, running her hands through his thick, dark hair. When their lips met again, she tightened her arms around him to ground herself.

At last they each settled back in their seats, fastened their seat belts, and Matt started the car. Pamela sighed deeply and turned halfway so she could continue to look at him, content in the knowledge that they had so much to discover about each other and all the time in the world to do it.

Coming Soon . . .
**Couples # 20**
*NO CONTEST*

"I wasn't kidding when I said I haven't done this since I was seven or eight," Eric said, pulling his skatelace tight with one hand and hanging on to the door of his cream-colored Mustang with the other. "I guess this is it," he said, pushing himself off from the car and across the paved lot. Instantly his legs shot out from under him.

"Watch it!" Katie cried, impulsively grabbing his hand before he could go down completely. His fingers closed tightly around hers. Katie felt sorry for Eric, and with her free hand patted his arm. "Don't worry. I won't let you fall," she said.

She patiently steered him to the path. The sidewalk, in spite of its cracks, was easier to skate on. They held hands the whole time, though by now Eric was skating more steadily.

"Let's see how you do on your own now." She skated a little ahead of him and turned around.

171

"Take it slowly," she warned as they turned the corner beneath the archway of trees. Her warning came too late.

Eric had sped up just a little, trying to catch up with her. All at once he lost his balance, and his legs began going out from under him. He reached for Katie. She reached for him. Together they tumbled into a deep pile of cherry blossoms.

"Are you okay?" Katie asked, trying to catch her breath. Eric had landed on top of her and knocked the wind out of her.

Eric's thick eyebrows arched up. "Sorry," he apologized, without letting go of her hands.

Katie sat very still, her legs sticking straight out in front of her, gazing right back into Eric's eyes. Everything seemed to stop: her heart, her thoughts, the sounds of the birds chirping overhead, even the cool breeze. Katie thought for a moment the world had stopped turning.